I0598917

DOWN
ICE
DIAMONDS

DOWN
ICE
DIAMONDS

A Story of Traveling Treasure

PAUL SHERBURNE

Published by Wilson Duke

Published by Wilson Duke

2017

Copyright © Paul Sherburne 2017

ISBN 978-0-9985386-8-6

CONTENTS

DEDICATION

This book is the result of my lifelong interest in earth science and a particular curiosity of cause and effect.

I owe a great deal of my knowledge and regard for the topic having studied Glacial Geology with Dr. Harold Borns, Professor Emeritus, Founder and Director, Climate Change Institute & School of Earth and Climate Sciences (formerly Institute for Quaternary Studies), University of Maine, 1974-1988.

Prologue

When questioned about his heritage in a scene in one of his films, (Will Rogers) informed a passport officer—who had inquired whether he was an American citizen—that his mother and father were both part Cherokee and he "was born and raised in Indian Territory. Course I'm not one of these Americans whose ancestors come over on the Mayflower, but we met 'em at the boat when they landed. And it's always been to the everlasting discredit of the Indian race that we ever let 'em land."

This passport office scene is from the 1930 Fox film, *So This Is London*. Rogers continued his soliloquy by reaffirming his statement in the face of scandalized expressions from a pair of onlookers: "It was," he said, referring to the discredit due the Indians for letting the Pilgrims land. "That's the only thing that I'd ever blame the Indians for."

The Papers of Will Rogers: The Early Years, by Will Rogers, Arthur Frank Wertheim, and Barbara Bair, pgs 31, 39.

2000 BCE

Near the Koksoak River, Ungava Bay region, Northern Quebec

"Is that tight enough?" asked 11-year-old Takubvik. "Yes, it should hold well," his father Oomailiq replied. Father and son had spent the afternoon repairing the lashings on a neighbor's qamutik (sled), using long, narrow strips of raw caribou hide. It is late fall in the Arctic region of northern Quebec.

They are in the summer Inuit village of Saimuk next to the Koksoak River, several miles upriver from Ungava Bay. On the way back to their family's sod hut, Oomailiq explains that the wet hide strips will shrink and tighten over the next several days.

Back in the hut, they strip to the waist and gather themselves on a polar bear rug covering most of the hut's central chamber to await their evening meal. While Aituserk, Takubvik's mother, prepares servings of salmon fillets and duck soup she is warming in soapstone bowls perched above a seal oil flame, Oomailiq leans his head closer to his only child and grasps his hands.

"I have decided to speak to the elders and tell them that you are now ready for adult duties," Oomailiq says, quietly and pridefully. This life-changing decision was what every young Inuk boy waited to hear. Takubvik looked up to his father and nodded his acceptance, his wide-eyed expression clearly revealing excitement over the elevation to this new status. Oomailiq knew from his own experience that his son's expression might well be masking a measure of underlying uncertainty.

Prepared for this, and to allay any feelings of doubt, Oomailiq was ready with a suggestion. "In the morning you will demonstrate that you are ready by performing a mock hunt, just as you have been taught," he said.

It was with this show of confidence that the 11-year-old was able to calm himself and enjoy his meal, but it was only when saw his parents smile proudly to each other with tears in their eyes that Takubvik was truly at ease.

He had some difficulty getting to sleep on his platform bed in a darkened corner of the sod hut, as might be expected, but he managed a good night's rest and awoke refreshed. Seeing his parents already up and about, he suppressed a grin, tossed his caribou hide blanket aside, and arose to face what would be a memorable day. While hurrying to dress, his mother Aituserk appeared and gently placing her roughened hands on his cheeks. She wisely cautioned him to take time to eat the bowl of caribou stew she had warmed for his morning meal before going outside. As an aside she added, "You should take your cousin along today."

He emerged from the narrow opening of a hut several minutes later to find himself standing in an endless, white landscape, created overnight by the first substantial snowfall of the changing season. It was a welcome sign that the time had arrived for the waters of the nearby Koksoak River to begin freezing. With heavier snows and dropping temperatures certain to follow, the river and nearby sea ice would soon become solid enough to support the heavily laden sleds of the twenty Inuit families of Saimuk on their annual trek north to winter quarters.

In just a few weeks, the entire community would leave their summer encampment to travel downriver and onto the sea ice covering Ungava Bay, moving northward until reaching the shoreline of Akpatok Island. There they would re-build their winter ice homes and continue a hunting tradition passed down from uncounted earlier generations. The men would harvest fur seals, an occasional walrus or a narwhale, while most of the women and older children would fish through ice holes cut nearer the shoreline.

Meanwhile, the time for hunting caribou west of the boreal

forestland surrounding the Koksoak's many feeder-rivers and streams had ended. Takubvik is pleased that he will be invited to join in the next season's hunt when the herd will once again pass through the territory. Today, however, to demonstrate his prowess and new status, he will travel unarmed to the land of the caribou and return safely.

Since it was only going to be a daytime mock hunt, he invites his little cousin along for the ride. He remembered something his mother had said, and thought, she wants me to show I'm capable of caring for others. He meets 8-year-old Uritsakatak at the sled dog tie-down, where they select a team of five dogs and string them to a light sled in preparation for the practice run along a familiar westward trail paralleling the River.

With a small group of elders silently observing from a polite distance, Oomailiq proudly watches over the preparations, satisfied with his son's display of skill, and pleased that his instructions are being followed. As practiced, in addition to a small sack of food for themselves and their animals, he noted that the youngsters tucked in a few items of winter clothing in the event the weather might unexpectedly change while they are away from the settlement.

By mid-day, Takubvik, with Uritsakatak riding in the sled, had traveled well inland, staying on higher ground as much as possible while keeping the River always in sight. They come upon an area where a number of shallow valleys run away to the west, the sides of which have been partially blown clear of snow and contain thin stands of black spruce and larch trees. Lichen, the caribou's favorite winter food, is prevalent over most of the open ground, and they see the scattered remains of summer grasses that supplied the wild herds on their southward migration. As they move closer, they spot a few cast-off antlers, and recognize clearly defined pathways in the tundra tramped down the padded hooves of endless numbers of caribou moving in trail.

They take the time to collect several antlers and load them onto the sled. They had begun their trip in light winds, but it had freshened substantially from the northwest, and the temperature was dropping rapidly. Deciding they had gone as far from their settlement as necessary, they spot a depression in the base of a long, gravel ridge that contains several, large boulders. After pausing to put on their winter parkas made of double-layered caribou skins, the hoods of which are lined with wolf fur, they anchor their dogs and settle into a cave-like space between two of the big boulders. After giving chunks of dried fish to the dogs, they huddle together out of the wind to rest and eat. They lean against the gravel bank and began chewing on strips of dried arctic hare.

"We have traveled far enough today," Takubvik says in his native Inuk tongue. "There are many caribou signs, and if I were on a hunt I'm sure I could take one."

"Yes," his younger cousin replies, and in a somber voice says, "but of course I wouldn't be allowed to be with you."

"No, but at least when I'm out with the other men, you will know where we are hunting and what the land looks like."

Uritsakatak turns to face her cousin, and is about to respond, when she giggles and says, "You have juice on your face."

Takubvik laughs and wipes his face with his hand, after which he casually sticks his fingers into the dry, sandy gravel next to his knee to clean them. He glances down at the gravel he has disturbed and notices several small stones standing out from the others. He picks out one of the larger ones and holds it up in the light. The nuggets are almost the color of snow.

"I've never seen these before," he says, wiping the stone between wetted fingers and then holding it up toward the opening.

"What is it?" Uritsakatak asks.

"I don't know, but when I hold it up to the sky it makes colors!"

"Let's take some back to the village," she says. "Maybe your father has seen them before, or perhaps my mother can find a use for them."

Their return journey was uneventful, and as soon as the sled is cared for and the dogs re-settled, they set about finding their parents to report on their adventure and to share their unexpected find—a handful of the most unusual stones they or anyone in their village have ever seen.

1000 BCE

Near the Pleasant River, East Branch of the Penobscot River, in central Maine

Twelve-year-old Namito is a Penawapskewi, a seasonally nomadic Tribe whose territory encompasses the Penobscot River Basin (in north-central Maine). Fall and winters find his Tribe well upriver, on the hunt for whitetail deer and moose and rabbits. The Tribe moves downriver to the Atlantic in the summer, working the mudflats for clams and tidal streams for salmon, and collecting the eggs of nesting birds along the rocky shore.[1]

Namito is greatly admired by the elders of his Tribe and so named for his ability to see clearly over great distances. Reed thin and unusually tall, Namito is especially adept at spotting game birds and deer, which are all but impossible to see when motionless. This morning, two moons after the river ice has broken up and been carried off, he is on his way to join his cousin Ahanu for a day of fishing in one of the northern feeder branches of the great River.

He is walking soundlessly along a well-used footpath next to the river toward an agreed upon meeting place when he spies a clutch of brightly colored wood ducks drifting on the current a short distance away from the shore. Carrying only a two-pronged fish spear and a

---

[1] The word "Penobscot" originates from a mispronunciation of their name "Penawapskewi". The word means "rocky part" or "descending ledges" and originally referred to the portion of the Penobscot River between Old Town and Bangor. Penobscots were members of the Algonquian people and belonged to the Abnaki confederacy. Penawahpskewi Indian Nation, PenobscotNation.Org

small knife, he is reduced to watching as the undisturbed waterfowl float by. He regrets not having brought his bow and arrow kit, because the highly prized feathers would have made a wonderful gift for his grandfather Tapkiau, and his Grandmother Loina could have used the meat to make more of her delicious duck soup.

The footpath he is following courses along the side of an esker, an extensive ridge running parallel to the river and composed of sand and gravel, the upper sides of which are now largely covered by all manner of trees, scrub brush and assorted wild grasses. The sloping side of the ridge between the path and the water is largely stripped of this growth by the annual freezing and thawing of the river's waters. The path he is on follows this boundary.

As Namito glances ahead, his attention is drawn to an unmoving shape that he instantly reads as out of place. Pausing, he studies the cluster of bushes halfway to the top of the ridge and quickly picks out the blink of a deer's eye amongst the leaves. Then, the tip of a huge rack is exposed when a leaf moves.

Ah, he thinks. *I see you, but this time you win. There's nothing to fear from this unarmed fisherman, at least on this morning.* He slowly reaches down, picks up a small stone, and tosses it in the direction of the animal. The large, mature buck spins away from the imagined threat and leaps up and over the ridge and is gone in an instant. It leaves in its wake a mini rockslide that brings a small ribbon of fresh gravel and stone to Namito's feet. His attention is instantly drawn to the bright reflection emanating from several small nuggets near the surface of the newly exposed gravel.

He steps closer to where the nuggets lay and, upon closer examination, finds them to be pieces of what look like milky, nearly colorless rocks. He is struck by how different they are from the surrounding rocks. What most impresses him is the way the sunlight reflects in many different colors and in different directions as he holds one of the larger nuggets up for closer examination. He gathers a dozen of the bright stones, thinking he will hide them for the time being and pick them up on his way back to his village. As he disturbs the surface, however, he realizes there are far more of the nuggets than he can carry at one time.

The small, ash creel he is carrying, he decides, will have to do for now, and puts several of the nuggets in it. He decides to return later, after fishing, and bring with him another, larger basket from the village. He carefully marks the location by arranging a small stack of larger rocks near some young cedar bushes next to where the slide ended. He is thinking that his grandmother and some of her friends will find the nuggets desirable and, perhaps, useful in some way.

A short while later, after joining his friend Ahanu, both boys venture out in the swiftly flowing but shallow river to a sandbar, which they know will get them closer to any passing salmon. By doing so, however, their scent is carried across the river, and on this morning directly into the noses of a huge, black sow bear and her two hungry year-old cubs. Suddenly, without warning, the animals lunge out of the brush, charge the boys, and are on them before they can escape. Their cries go unheard as both boys are quickly caught and mauled to death.

Moreville, Present Day

Near the Pleasant River, East Branch, in central Maine

For Mel Johnson, this summer is memorable for two reasons: he will turn 15 near the end of the season and finally be old enough to get his driver's license; and he will land his first, real paying job. It's not that he hasn't worked before, you understand, but cleaning his grandmother's basement, or helping a neighbor build a garage, while it might bring in a dollar or two, these are simple one-time tasks. Now, at last, he can stand proudly among his peers and display his own, real pay stub.

He is thrilled about getting this job at the Mayer Farm because it requires driving a tractor, and any job that includes driving is considered by him and his pals to be the absolute best. Ok, so in between the times of actual driving there will be hours of manual labor, heavy lifting, dirt, sweat, blisters, and sunburn, as well as long stretches of pure boredom. No matter. No problem. He is about to be elevated from adolescent doldrums to the world of grownups—where real motor vehicle operators sit behind the wheel.

It was a step, and an important one, in the growing up process. He isn't yet old enough to drive over the road, legally anyway. He can still tell his friends, truthfully, that yes, he worked all day driving a tractor. No need to mention all the other stuff, the picking up trash, limbs, junk, and other remaining detritus from the spring runoff littering farmer Mayer's otherwise beautiful grassy hayfields. And he also can omit mention that while doing all that driving, he will never actually leave that farm property, or that his time on the road, measured in fractions of minutes, will be spent crossing rather than traveling along that familiar paved surface.

Perhaps more importantly, the job won't be limited to cleaning up the fields. By mid-summer, hay will be cut, raked into rows, dried in the sun, and baled. Mel will help picking up those bales and loading them onto a trailer, where they will be stacked and later sold. Meanwhile, if he demonstrates that he can do his job responsibly, he might get to operate the hay rake. He decides without hesitation that he will so demonstrate.

By mid-July, most of the fields are cleared of river-born winter trash and haying is well under way. One very warm morning, while waiting for the uncut hay to dry out from overnight rain showers, Mel is tasked with finishing a small chore at the back end of the property, well out of sight of the farmhouse and roadway and perhaps two hundred yards from the nearby Pleasant River. Following instructions from Mr. Mayer, a small amount of debris gathered under some trees had been discovered and needs to be picked up.

He hooks the utility trailer to the smallish Fordson tractor and heads for the field, which requires a crossing of the road in front of the main farmhouse. As he checks both ways for oncoming traffic, his attention is drawn as it always is to a set of ramshackle buildings and dilapidated mobile home trailers that are clustered together a short distance away to his right on the opposite side of the road. The buildings are surrounded on three sides by dense woods, which separates them from the adjacent field toward which Mel is headed.

The assembly of structures is home to an extended family named Webber. Among the clan is a girl named Marie, who is one of Mel's classmates at school. She is way smarter than anyone else in the class. Nothing less than A ever graces her report card—starting with kindergarten. She absorbs lessons or reading assignments as naturally and as easily as others breathe air.

The Webbers are disparagingly referred to by many locals as

the 'swamp angels,' although Mel has always been embarrassed when people use the label, and more so when he hears his own parents employ it. While the Webbers might be among the most impoverished of anyone else in town, they aren't alone and certainly no angels— more than one of the male adults has had run-ins with the local game warden, and where they live is merely lowland and not a real swamp. The label is dubious in his mind. The real meaning of the derisory term is beyond his understanding. While many town-folk apply it to the clan with a broad brush, in his mind Marie is the exception.

During the slow ride to the rear of the field along the line of fencing separating the field from the woods behind the Webber property, Mel thinks about Marie. He wouldn't call her cute, like some of the other girls in his school, but to him, she's pretty enough, and definitely more physically advanced than her classmates. She's tall, wears her dark hair in long braids, and although he's never told anyone—even his closest friends, he likes her, and certainly envies her smarts.

He recalls when they were alone, together, for the first time. It was a late, fall day, and their third-grade teacher had taken ill shortly after lunchtime. The Principal decided the thing to do was end their school day early, and he sent the students home. The majority lived within walking distance, but Mel and Marie and one or two others had to wait for a school bus. The two of them passed the time on the steps at one of the side entrances where they had a view of one of the three rivers that passed through the town.

Conversation turned to the weather, and the upcoming winter, and Marie spoke about how that river, and the other two — one of which passed close to her home, would become frozen solid. And, of course, come spring, that ice would break free and jam into itself further downstream. That and the increased meltwater runoff would cause flooding, threatening their homestead, and litter their fields with junk wood and other detritus, just as it did every year.

"Last year, we found several tied-together bundles of really good boards near our yard that most likely came from the mill upriver. I thought we were going to keep them, but old Uncle Johnny said first we needed to talk to the owner."

"Why did he say that?" Mel asked. "I mean, finders keepers. Right?"

"Well," Marie replied, "He decided that the right thing to do, after we found the owner, was to offer to return them. Sure, we could have said nothing, and kept them all, and they were pretty good boards, probably worth a lot of money. Johnny was pretty sure that the owner would let us keep some — maybe as many as half of them, just because we reported their discovery."

"And, did that happen?"

"Yes, it did, and Johnny agreed to return the other half to the mill. He said it was the right thing to do: to share. We were able to build a new woodshed out of what we kept for ourselves."

"So, I guess that's why you were smiling so much when Mrs. Worthington said this morning that she was going to teach us about sharing. 'Course, she got sick, so I suppose we'll have to wait for her version."

———

Eventually, Mel reaches a small stand of spruce trees and catches a glimpse of the offending trash protruding from under low-hanging boughs. The hay in this part of the field hadn't yet been cut, and it is well over two feet high. He pulls the trailer up beside the trees and parks in a good position to load the wood. It is then that he notices more debris scattered beyond the trees out into the standing hay. Not easily seen from even a short distance away, he knows it can do serious damage to the delicate teeth on the mower's sickle blade.

Mel's thoughts are interrupted when the swirl of a light breeze brings with it the sound of children laughing and playing. The noise is clearly coming from the nearby woods, but when Mel looks toward the woods he sees no one. Stepping to the opposite side of the spruce trees he recognizes a familiar pathway leading into the woods beyond the fence. He knows the short pathway eventually leads to the field behind the Webber property, because two years ago he was bird hunting along this same tree line with a nephew of farmer Mayer and they discovered the trail while tracking a wounded partridge. In the opposite direction the trail crosses the Mayer field and leads to the River, and to some gravel ridges near the water. Two hundred feet or so into the woods the pathway widens into a clearing, in the center of which is a large puddle. The clearing is in heavy shadow, so he walks up to the fence to get a better view.

Mel smiles at the sight of four, squealing, naked youngsters, a mix of boys and girls ages six or seven, he guesses. They are chasing each other in a circle and running through the shallow water, making as much splash as they can, covering their bodies with the warm mud and obviously having a grand time. Mel surmises they are a mix of Webber kids with a visiting cousin or two along for the fun. Then, off to one side in shadow, he notices his friend and classmate Marie, standing quietly and apparently watching over the little ones as they frolic about. Moments later she turns her head and catches sight of Mel standing at the fence line. For several seconds, the two of them look directly at each other. Neither move, or attempt a wave, or nod their head in mutual recognition. It doesn't seem necessary, after all.

Then, suddenly, without turning away or changing expression, Marie gets naked. In a flash, she pulls her T-shirt off over her head and pushes her shorts and underpants down to the ground. Then, as her expression briefly morphs into a mischievous grin, she turns her head away and joins her four charges in the moving circle as they all continue their game in the mud puddle.

Mel remains motionless, uncertain if what he just saw happen really did happen. It is only when the sound of Marie's and the kid's squeals and splashing feet reach him that he realizes it did. Yes, it did. It really did. Sakes alive!

The Farm Retreat

Outside Madison, Wisconsin

It is an early spring afternoon month's later and thousands of miles away in south central Wisconsin, when Marie is wakened from a short nap by the sound of the shed door closing. She is dressed in an oversized sweatshirt, warm-up pants, and calf-length socks. As she sits up on the sofa and places her feet on the carpet in front of the sofa, her Aunt Ellie Webber steps into the kitchen and places two, large paper shopping bags on the counter.

"Oh, I see you're awake," her Aunt Ellie said.

"Yes. How long was I asleep?"

"About an hour," came the reply. "You feeling ok?"

"Just tired, I guess. Otherwise fine. I think I'll check on Charlie," Marie answered, referring to her 6-months-old son, whom she had put down for his nap a short while earlier. She stepped quietly to his crib and found him sleeping peacefully.

Returning to the kitchen, Marie said, "He's good for now. You need any help with those groceries?"

"No, thanks. You sit right there. It'll only take me a minute. You want something hot to drink? Tea, maybe?"

"Sounds good."

A few minutes later, Aunt Ellie placed a steaming cup of tea on a coffee table in front of the sofa and then eased herself into a nearby recliner with her own cup in hand.

"I think it's time we had a talk about your future, Marie. You've got to decide what you want to do with your life. Please understand, you can stay here as long as you like—you and your son, of course. But perhaps you ought to be thinking about finishing school. You could enroll right here in town for the fall session."

"Yes, I suppose you're right. I had to drop out after my junior year," Marie replied in an unsure voice. "I mean, I had no choice after that son-of-a-bitch raped me and I found myself pregnant."

"And, if I recall, that son-of-a-bitch was your cousin Roland? Who often visited and was accepted as part of the extended family?"

"Yes, it was. He's a Penobscot. Lives on the Indian Island Reservation down in Old Town. I guess I never did understand how we got to be related."

"I do know, and if you want, I'll tell you. It was your mother who gave me the background. I'm surprised she never told you about it. It's something we talked about when we were much younger and I was still living back there in Maine. You know how sisters share secrets, I suppose."

"Yes, I do. Of course."

"Well, let me see if I have this straight. You never knew your father, did you?"

"No. Mother refused to discuss it."

"Ok. Your mother met your father up in Houlton. She was in high school at the time, and was taken in by some distant relatives up there during the fall potato harvest. They were part Indian themselves, from the Maliseet Tribe. You may not know, but the Maliseet Tobique Reservation in New Brunswick is just across the border and not far away.

The Maliseets are noted for moving back and forth across the border, just as they have done for untold centuries, to find work and to hunt and fish. Apparently, your mother and one of the young studs from that tribe ended up working beside each other during the potato harvest. He was handsome, smart, and seemed like a nice young man. They struck up a friendship that turned into, well, you know ... anyway, your mother got pregnant. The two of them might have had other plans, but when the young man's family learned what had happened, his father showed up and took him back across the border, barring him from ever crossing again. Sadly, she never saw him after that."

"I guess I'm not surprised about that, but how did I get to be cousins with the family on the Island?"

"The Penobscots and the Maliseets are known for their fondness for travel. In the old days, it was by canoe and by foot, chasing the seasons from the coastal outlets to the wetlands of the wintery north. They still spend some time together, whether it's for ceremonial functions or to share in the resources they both have access to. There is mixed blood all over the State of Maine, and even I knew about some of the family's cousins down in Old Town," Aunt Ellie answered. "And, like it or not, as you already have Native American blood, your son will have some, too. It may not mean much, at the moment, but sometime in the future being of Native American heritage could be an important advantage."

Marie thought about that for a few moments, and then she said, recalling that horrible night, "One of them showed up that spring of my junior year, and just moved in. My mother said he could stay and help out. He was supposed to be a mechanic, and we sure needed that kind of help, with everything half broken down most of the time. His name was Roland, and he was already pretty big and strong. I thought he was nice enough, and he was kept busy, so I didn't spend a lot of time with him, but I guess he was watching me all the while ... biding his time, apparently.

Then there was that one, horrible night about three months before the end of school. I had gone to bed. Suddenly, Roland and my other cousin Willis came in, jumped on me and started pulling off my nightgown. It was pitch dark, so I couldn't see their faces, but I guessed who it was. I did the best I could to fight them, but together they were just too strong. They held a corner of the blanket over my mouth, threatening me to be quiet and not tell anyone or I would be hurt. It was awful. I cried all night long after it was over.

After I was raped, and I know it was Roland who did it because I scratched his face, and the next day I could see the marks. I expected they might take turns, but Willis was too scared to join in. He ran off and left Roland to himself."

"And, so, after you knew you were pregnant, you had no choice but to leave school and come out here to have your baby. I recall that you were doing well in school. Did you have any special friends there? Did they know what happened?"

"I was so embarrassed I didn't go back for the fall term. Not long after the start of the school year, I was in town with my mother and her niece Gladys ... you know, the kid who was born with brain damage ... the one people in town always joked about, calling her a 'swamp angel' and brushing all of us with that label ... and I was already sticking out pretty good, so anyone who saw me could put two and two together as to why I left school. I'm sure the rumors were flying."

"I remember coming out of the drug store one day in the fall, right across the street from the bank, and the only one of my classmates who saw me, before I left town to come out here to your farm, was Mel Johnson. Although he was in his brother's pickup and tried to not let on, I know he saw me. And I pretended I hadn't seen him. He was about the only one in the whole class whom I respected. We weren't what you might call close friends, exactly, but we were both good students and took a lot of the same classes. I guess of all my classmates, I remember him the most."

"I know the Johnson family," Aunt Ellie said. "They were very well thought of in town."

"Yes, they were good people. Mel worked one or two summers on a farm right across the road from our place," Marie replied, thinking back to a day when she and some kids splashed about in a mud puddle.

Coming of Age

Back on the small farm outside Madison, Wisconsin

Much has changed over the decade following the arrival of a young, very pregnant Marie at her Aunt Ellie's small farm. Ellie had run the farm single-handedly after the untimely death of her husband from brain cancer more than fifteen years earlier. A year after the birth of her son, Charlie, Marie took her Aunt's advice and enrolled in the local high school, graduating near the top of her class. Her high school yearbook photo revealed her to be a raven-haired, attractive young woman. Taller than average, she was well tanned and in excellent physical shape from all the hard work she was doing on her Aunt's farm.

Now, Marie, her ten-year-old son Charlie, and her Aunt Ellie are returning to the farm outside Madison in the early evening of a cool, June day. They have been on the road for just over three hours, leaving the Law School on 60th Street in downtown Chicago less than an hour after Marie was awarded her J.D. degree in Public Interest Law. Prior to entering the Law School, Marie completed her Bachelor's Degree in History, summa cum laude, at the University of Wisconsin in Madison. It had taken her only three years, taking advantage of what the school called its flexible scheduling option.

She had relied on scholarships and grants to get through her undergraduate program, which she easily qualified for, and while committing herself to a substantial loan to pay for graduate school, she planned to look into work with a human rights organization, or one of several non-profits, through the Law School's loan repayment assistance program. Her intent was to become debt free as soon as possible.

"That was a very nice affair, Marie," Aunt Ellie said, as they entered the kitchen. "I'm so pleased for you. Sorry that your mother Ollie didn't live long enough to see this day. She would have been so proud of you."

While Marie was mid-way through Law School, she received a letter from a cousin back in Maine, informing her that her mother Ollie had unexpectedly been found dead. She had apparently been living with a Canadian logger somewhere in New Brunswick, well off the grid, and one cold night had wandered off alone. What was left of her body was found months later. There was no funeral service to attend, and Marie got over the news a short time later.

"She might have been," Marie replied, "but I don't think she ever understood what finishing school and going to college means. Much less Law School. No one did back home, except for people like old Uncle Johnny—I'd give him the benefit of the doubt. He was never one to talk much, and I'm guessing he was the only one who appreciated that I had a brain. I also think he might have regretted what happened to me, which he never talked about, of course. Anyway, anyway, thank you for being such a terrific stand-in today."

"How about you, Charlie," aunt Ellie said. "You must be proud of your mother."

"Sure am," he replied. "Didn't notice any other single Moms up there on that platform today."

"You were telling me about maybe working up in Canada," aunt Ellie said. "Anything more on that?"

"As you know, my legal specialty in Public Interest Law comes with provision that allows me to work for a non-profit, or an NGO, or any organization like that as a way of forgiving a good part of my school loan. Recently, a lady in the placement office called me to her office. She had an idea about me putting together a grant request.

It was kind of funny the way it happened. I mean, she asked me if I would be willing to work with aboriginals. I said, 'certainly,' not knowing what she had in mind, but then she got all embarrassed. She blushed and said, 'oh, I didn't mean just because of your background.' Seems she had noted that on my application for law school I had checked the Native American box on the ethnic background item."

"Well, you are part Indian," aunt Ellie replied.

"Yes, as it so happens. Anyway, she regained her composure and went on to explain that there are some new developments going on in Maine with the Native Americans and that they could use the help of someone with my legal training. She also said there are many of the same things going on in Quebec with their Inuit and Cree aboriginals. I'll have to put together a grant proposal, which she said they would help me with, and then she gave me a list of reference materials and a bibliography to research. I have a month to do all that work and then we'll see what develops."

"Could be quite a challenge," Aunt Ellie said.

"Yes, I suspect it will be," Marie replied.

The Re-Discovery

Near the Pleasant River, East Branch of the Penobscot River, in Central Maine

87-year-old Old John "Johnny" Webber became the clan's patriarch upon the death of his older sister Mable, who died a month earlier just days shy of reaching age 91. It is late fall and all signs point to an unusually nasty winter ahead, so Johnny has put out the word that he wants all the youngsters available for a weekend project. He has told them it is important they be ready for a little hard work.

The tar-paper shacks and broken down trailers that make up the Webber homestead next to the river are in their usual state of disrepair, but at least the roofs are patched up, and the few, whole storm windows that could be found have been installed. The main thing left to do is to stock up enough wood to get them through the coming cold season.

On that Saturday morning, with Johnny sitting in his overstuffed chair next to a Franklin stove in his doublewide, four young boys are lined up facing him on a broken down sofa. Two are his grandsons: Edgar and Sam Webber; one is a grand nephew, Norm Williams; and one is a distant cousin of someone in the clan by the name of Trent Gilbertson. All are young teenagers. None has the reputation of being particularly energetic or self-motivated, but the old man understands that this crew is all he has to work with. He regrets that his granddaughter Marie is no longer around to take charge of this gang of misfits.

"Alright, boys," he says, "we got us a little job to do. Word is, we're going to have a really hard winter ahead, and there's six woodpiles that need to be stocked up. You know I can't get out myself anymore, so you'll have to do the job. We're going to need some hardwood and some kindling, and I know just where you'll find it. This weekend you'll concentrate on kindling. This is what you need to do," he begins, and details exactly where the boys are to look.

————————

The four boys head out in a doodlebug, a machine that had once been a Model A Ford and was now an ugly looking flatbed truck with no cab. An old crate serves as a driver's seat. After a short ride toward the river, they come across some scattered wood in a field that they quickly collect and toss onto the vehicle's bed.

A half hour later, having run out of anything worth collecting, they park the doodlebug near the river at the base of a gravel ridge.

Walking north along the river, they reach an area with numerous downed trees that have dried in the sun. Each of them begins dragging the wood back to their vehicle.

"Hey, I see some more over here," Edgar Webber yelled to his younger brother Sam, calling out from the river-facing side of the long gravel ridge. They are working their way along the ridge following the plan outlined by old Johnny. He had told them that the spring floods always left behind a lot of driftwood, and it always made great kindling.

Edgar approached a small pile of what had once been cedar trees, which is just what he was looking for. Sam pulled the remains of a smallish tree out of the pile and headed back down the ridge.

"Norm and Trent should be back at the buggy. Tell them to give us a hand here when you see them."

Edgar is the biggest of the four and decides to unsnarl the pile and spread it out so the other three will be able to haul it out to be loaded. After several minutes, he has recovered all that is worth keeping when he recognizes that the one last tree in his hand is anchored by its roots into the ridge. He tugs and pulls, swinging it back and forth several times, but it refuses to come out.

Just then Sam and the other two boys return.

"Hey, Norm, Trent. Grab on over here and help me pull," Edgar ordered. The three are straining on the small tree when Sam moves closer to the root to see if he can see why it won't come loose.

"This thing's never going to come out," he said, seeing a tangle of sizable roots projecting well into the ground. "We'll have to get an axe if we want to keep it."

"Nah," Edgar replied, easing his pull as did the other two boys. "There are too many others like it that don't have stuck roots."

As they were about to leave and look for more wood, Sam said, "What's this?" He had spotted what looked like the partial remains of an old basket in the dirt between the roots.

Edgar, Trent and Norm step closer. "Looks like some kind of basket," Trent says. He climbs down to the root ball to get a closer look. "I think it might be a creel, or maybe a small pack basket. Made of ash, most likely. Pretty old, too." He tests the woven wood, finding it quite fragile.

"Could it be Indian?" Sam asked.

"Might be. Same weave as I've seen on Penobscot baskets."

"What d'ya want to do wiff it?" Norm questioned.

"There's a potato sack on the buggy," Edgar replied. "I'll bring it back on our next trip and we'll take the basket back to old Johnny. Maybe he'll know something about it."

By mid-afternoon, the boys had managed to gather a substantial load on the buggy's flatbed. They tie it on with an assortment of old ropes and head back to the homestead, pleased with their efforts. At Edgar's feet is a potato sack, in which rests the remains of an aged, small wood basket, with whatever is inside remaining untouched.

When they return, they to go the doublewide and find Johnny apparently sound asleep in his old chair. Rather than wake him, they spend the next half hour unloading the buggy. As they are pulling off the last of the wood the sky suddenly darkens, the wind picks up, and in minutes the rain starts—quickly turning into a full-blown thunderstorm.

Trent grabs the potato sack and runs into a nearby shed, where he tosses it into a corner. Right behind him, Norm rushes in and crashes clumsily into his friend. The two of them tussle in play fight, knocking things off the wall and kicking things around on the floor. In the brief scuffle a wood shelf cum-workbench is unhinged and falls to the floor—covering the sack.

Eventually the rain and wind ease, and the boys go to the doublewide to report on their wood-collecting work. They are immediately hit with a foul odor, and make jokes about how the old man must have shit his pants. They quickly find out, however, that Johnny is not in fact asleep: he had taken his last breath, apparently suffering a stroke, or maybe a heart attack, right in his chair next to the stove—probably while the boys were horsing around out in the woodshed.

From that point on, as the boys and others of the clan cope with Johnny's death, the potato sack and the mysterious basket it contained are ignored and soon forgotten. It is a few months afterward that the property is abandoned as everyone moves on to live with nearby relatives and begin new lives elsewhere.

Earlier Times in the Far North

Northern Quebec Province, near Ungava Bay

To the uninformed, the barren interior landscape of Quebec Province north of the 55th parallel has little to offer. This remarkable area encompasses one third of the entire Province—surrounded by water on three sides and geographically equal in size to France, Germany and Spain, combined; where trees are all but absent; where Arctic conditions prevail nine months of the year; and where the aboriginal population of 9,000 Inuit and 5,000 Cree reside in one of fourteen remote villages scattered along its extensive coastline. There are no connecting roads between villages, and none transect the interior. On sleds pulled by dogs, however, the Nunavumiut have[2] survived for thousands of years as hunters and fishers and trappers, learning how to travel in this trackless wilderness.

In addition to the Amerindian population, the area (in recent times called Nunavik) is home to numerous creatures on the ground, in the air and in the water, including marine mammals such as ringed and bearded seal, walrus, polar bear, and beluga and killer whales. On land there are brown bear, musk-oxen, caribou, Arctic fox, and wolverines. Winged creatures include Canadian geese, eider duck, peregrine falcon, gyrfalcon, rough-legged hawk, snowy owl, and ptarmigan. And, finally: there is the Atlantic and landlocked salmon; sea-run, brook and lake trout; and finally Arctic char, populating its

2   An additional 4,500 Cree reside in one of four interior communities in the southern region of Quebec

waters.

The northernmost reaches of the Province are geographically arranged in the shape of a mitten-covered left hand. A large body of water called Ungava Bay separates the thumb and fingers while the Straits connecting the Atlantic and the Gulf of Labrador with Hudson Bay surround the fingertips. Hudson Bay itself lies to the west (left of the little finger). The land on the thumb's inside edge belongs to Quebec, while the land outside and extending down the wrist (south) belongs to Newfoundland-Labrador. The Torngat Mountains and the Torngat Mountain National Park, share the landmass of the thumb.

In light winds, near-freezing temperature, and hazy early-morning sunlight, two hunters track steadily northward, the two dog teams and lightly loaded sleds gliding smoothly in-trail. It is the beginning days of the winter season and the surface is fully snow-covered, making for easy travel. They have been on the move for over three days and will eventually travel nearly 300 miles before reaching their destination at the village of Quaqtaq on the western shore of Ungava Bay. (The location would be comparable to the fingernail on the first finger of the left hand inside a mitten.)

Aani Oovaut and his friend Minialuk Papak began their trip from their homes in Kuujjuaq, located on the western shore of the Koksoak River and surrounding a former WWII-era airfield known as Crystal I. The airfield was constructed and operated by the US Army Airforce as part of its northern line of defense.

Previously, their village was located on the river's eastern shore, closer to Ungava Bay, and called Saimuk. Its population was much smaller, and served for centuries as a summertime village for aboriginal hunters and trappers. A short distance away from the village and in the early 19th Century, the Hudson's Bay Company set up a Trading Post and traded furs and skins with the people of Saimuk. In the mid-19th Century, both the village and the Trading Post were relocated upstream and to the opposite shore on land adjacent to the airfield. The village was re-named Kuujjuaq and grew to become one of the Nunavik's largest. The Trading Post eventually went out of business.

Along their northward journey, the two young men paused for overnight stops in the villages of Tasiujaq, Aupulak, and Kangirsuk, located along the western shore of the Bay. These pleasurable visits allowed the men and their dogs a rest as well as an opportunity to absorb the latest news about fishing and hunting and to maintain relations with kinfolk. They crest a small ridge at the base of a small peninsula jutting into Ungava Bay's western shore, giving them a view of the hunting grounds they and their families have worked for generations.

Their destination, the village of Quaqtaq, lies ahead and to their right, on the western side of the peninsula and only a few more hours' travel away. Some considerable distance away, to their left, they can see Diana Island in the Strait, and well off in the distance to the east, they catch sight of Akpatok, a much larger island in Ungava Bay. They know that in a few weeks, the entire area will ice over and remain frozen until the next summer, giving them access to both islands.

———

After running parallel to the shoreline for several minutes and with a quick hand signal by Aani, the men simultaneously stomp on their sled's anchor-brake and call their dogs to a halt. Minialuk, traveling in the rear, walks forward to stand next to his friend. After being on the move for many hours, the two men wordlessly enjoy spending the next several minutes scanning the open waters, looking for telltale signs of beluga waterspouts or puffs of warm seal or walrus breath in the icy, dark blue waters. They have come to the area for the annual beluga hunt, anticipating the return trip home laden with a winter-long supply of meat, bones, and blubber to share with their friends and families.

With no clear sightings, not surprising to either man, they soon move on toward the village, anxious to connect with their fellow hunters and engage in the preparations for the annual harvest. By noon, they reach the village and are greeted by their respective family relatives.

After arranging for the care and feeding of their dogs, and tending to their sleds, the men and their elders move inside, where they quickly find a place in their respective family circles. Before moving onto the frozen sea and setting up winter hunting quarters, they will spend the next ten days to two weeks here, sharing each other's warmth and companionship.

In the home of his uncle, near the village's center, Aani enjoys a lunch of Arctic hare stew and boiled duck eggs and settles onto a fur-lined platform near the stove with his cup of tea. In the dim light of a seal oil lamp, his Uncle Maaki brings him up to date on the latest beluga sightings and hunting plans, after which the conversation shifts to current affairs and concerns—the most newsworthy being the increase in traffic to the area by southerners.

"You say many southerners have been here? Do you know why they are coming?" Aani asked in his native Inuit language.

"My friend Henry, who works out at the airport, says he overheard one of the men say they are here to look at the rocks and other things in the ground. He thinks they are certain there are valuable stones to be found," Uncle Maaki replied.

"Yes. I heard the same thing from a friend back in Kuujjuaq. He, too, works at the local airport, and said several small groups of men flew in and then traveled by boat and overland out east to Kangiqsujuaq and then on to the Torngat Mountains. There was some talk of finding evidence, right there on the ground near one of the larger fjords, but to collect enough material to confirm their sightings of minerals they decided they would need more time and special equipment," Aani said.

"How do you feel about these southerners traveling around in our hunting grounds?" Uncle Maaki asked.

"Unnnggh," Aani grunted. "I think it is wrong and I don't like it. I am also troubled that they feel no obligation to ask for permission to run about on our lands, or to help themselves to samples of our ground. I heard talk about a group from an oil company coming to test for oil and gas beneath our homelands—well into the interior as well as off shore where the whales live. And, now that I think about it, there is supposed to be some people coming with motor sleds and much equipment—right up here to Quaqtaq, in the next few months. They have their eye on the big holes in the ground in the interior, to the west, where mother Earth is said to have swallowed giant objects that fell from the sky. Many of these objects are said to contain valuable things."

"Yes, we heard about that, too," Uncle Maaki responded. "We discussed it at our elder's council, but we concluded that there was little we could do about it. And, as we finished that discussion, the conversation turned to complaints about the choice many of our younger hunters are making—to give up hunting for the season to work as guides and laborers for these southerners."

"Are you talking about the lands where we often go to harvest caribou? In the land of the round valleys?" Aani asked.

"Yes. That's the very place."

"Unnnggh. That is not good."

The Plan for Quebec

At the University Inn, downtown Montreal, Canada

It is a cool spring morning a few years later when 34-year-old Mel Johnson walks into the restaurant at the University Inn in downtown Montreal, a familiar establishment and one of his favorites north of the border. He has come for an 8 o'clock breakfast meeting with Jon Martin, Chief Planning Officer for the Northpipe Corporation, whose headquarters are in Alberta Province in western Canada. A contract has been worked out between Mel's firm and Northpipe, and only a few final details need to be settled.

Mel is a consulting engineer, and the owner and manager a small, four-man firm, called Johnson & Associates, headquartered in Marblehead, Massachusetts. Their core business is providing technical advice on the design requirements, routings, costs, and maintenance plans for oil and natural gas lines.

The invitation to meet at the Inn on Prince Arthur Street, which was in close proximity to McGill University, was taken by Mel to mean good news for his firm's reputation, having come from one of Canada's major energy corporations. Based on his reading of the materials provided earlier by Mr. Martin's office, the project holds promise to be a game-changer for his firm and its partners.

The B&B location was agreed to by both men, both for its familiarity and charm and its proximity to McGill University's Earth and Planetary Science Center. Mel had served on occasion as an adjunct faculty member at the Center, using the B&B as his temporary residence. Some others on his team had done the same over the past few years. Jon Martin had come to the city a few days earlier for meetings with government officials involved with Plan Nord, Canada's a major economic development strategy for northern Quebec.

After a warm welcome by the Inn's host, Mel explained that he was expecting another gentleman to join him. He was shown to a vacant booth, and a waitress promptly appeared to deliver an iced-container of fresh-squeezed orange juice and a coffee urn. After serving himself, Mel glanced toward the lobby and spotted Jon Martin arriving. Jon was a half-foot shorter than Mel, perhaps twenty years older, and was dressed in a navy blazer with gray slacks, and a blue necktie sporting his corporation's logo. The two men greeted each other at the booth, and after insisting on the use of first names, they walked together to the buffet table to select their breakfast choices. Eggs, fries and ham for Mel, and French toast and bacon for Roy.

Mel was fully knowledgeable about Northpipe's involvement in pipeline operations, transporting oil and natural gas resources originating in the western provinces across southern Canada. Before coming to Northpipe over a year ago, Jon had worked for several years on energy development and pipeline operations in Europe as well as the Middle East. He quickly became recognized as a leading figure in the Canadian energy field.

As requested, Mel had brought extra copies of his resume as well as those of his partners, which included: John Jenkins, a highly skilled infrastructure and pipeline materials expert; Billy Poulin, who wrote the book on petroleum transport and storage; and Eddy Burns, a leading expert on oil and gas exploration and drilling. Each partner visits the Marblehead headquarters from time to time, but most of the time they operated out of home offices. Usually all four get together for a few days about every three months.

As they were enjoying their breakfast, the talk turned to backgrounds and experiences. Mel explained that he had enlisted in the Coast Guard immediately after high school, specializing in

Electronics and Hydrographic Survey (ocean bottom mapping). Following his military service, he was awarded a scholarship to attend the Massachusetts Institute of Technology, where he earned a degree in Material Science and Engineering. Later, he added an MBA degree from Harvard. He noted that the firm's partners were also highly qualified, with degrees from such places as Cornell, Stanford, and Texas Tech., and all had extensive in-the-field-with-hands-on experiences throughout the U.S. and abroad. Like Mel, they too often were invited to serve from time to time as adjunct faculty at McGill.

Mel is a trim six-footer, with a full head of blonde hair and a hint of gray in his sideburns. He is unmarried, although less than a decade earlier, while on a trip to Quebec City, seeking to expand the business further after opening a subsidiary office in Portland, Maine office, he met and fell in love with an attractive young woman who was the daughter of a Canadian client.

Claudette Marquis was a highly skilled medical research specialist and in the beginning stages of a promising career at Quebec City's Jeffrey Hale Hospital. Following a courtship that lasted only a few months, they decided to get married and were in the process of deciding where to make their home—in Canada or in the US, when Claudette was tragically run down by a drunk driver while walking home on Avenue Holland. She died in the ambulance on the trip back to the Hospital.

Both families were stunned, and it was some time before Mel recovered from the tragedy. Although meeting and forming a close bond with several young women later on, he found himself more than occupied with growing his business and too little time available to seriously consider marrying and settling down. He buried himself in his work, opening two more branch offices, while at the same time learning to enjoy his freedom, the travel involved, and the exposure to new and exciting challenges.

With their meal finished, they quickly got down to business. Jon said, "The leadership of our corporation was most impressed with your firm's record and reputation in this industry. We are pleased to have you on board with us." And for the next several minutes, he discussed his meetings on Plan Nord with the Ministry for Natural Resources.

"Plan Nord is a 25 year-long commitment on the part of the Canadian government. In support of that effort, our company has been granted the rights to develop oil and natural gas pipeline routes from northern Quebec to transport terminals and refineries on the St. Lawrence River in Quebec City." He laid out a map of northern Canada, and pointed to the province of Quebec.

"What we'll be doing is truly planning outside the box. In the arctic seabed and under any number of inner-arctic islands, lies one-fifth of the world's oil and natural gas reserves. Based on test data, the most likely areas include the Davis Strait and Cumberland Sound to the east of Baffin Island, and the Hudson Strait, to the south. The seabed around Quebec, from Ungava Bay to the Hudson Bay itself, is still awaiting full exploration, although that whole topic is somewhat controversial for reasons explained in the materials sent to your earlier.[3]

Now, let's suppose that sometime in the future, drilling rights are awarded and those oil and gas reserves are recovered. How will the product be delivered for refinement? Presently, there is only one existing option: transport by ship around Newfoundland Labrador to the St. Lawrence Seaway into Quebec City during the ice-free months of the year. This is where you and your team enter the picture.

We're thinking of northern Quebec as the primary collection point for the entire operation. This would serve a dual purpose: first, to collect the raw product much closer to the source, substantially reducing ship transport requirements; and, second, function as the head of a pipeline system to deliver that product directly to the Quebec City refineries. Your initial task will be to identify the most desirable locations for such a collection point — or points, if necessary.

To make this all work, there are several major issues to be resolved, not the least of which is the matter of rights to the seabed and the oil and gas reserves themselves. You see, the recent passage of

3   1.9 billion barrels (300×106 m3) of oil and 19.8 trillion cubic feet (560×109 m3) of natural gas

the Nunavut Land Claims Settlement Act, covering the eastern portion of what has historically been known as the Northwest Territories, presents a challenge to — and perhaps an opportunity for, Quebec, and for this project. Under the terms of that agreement, Nunavut's coastal boundaries extend to the high tide mark around the shoreline of Quebec as well as the provinces of Ontario and Manitoba. That means that all the waters of Hudson Bay around to Ungava Bay belong not to Quebec, but to the Nunavut. Thus, at present, Quebec, Ontario and Manitoba are left with no rights to the development of their own coastal seabed.

———

That fact is being challenged and may well change in the future, but in the interim our planning strategy will be to find a way to achieve cooperation between the Nunavut and the province of Quebec, with the Nunavik strategically located between the two. Now, as you can see from this map, there are a number of Inuit settlements along the coastline of Nunavik, none of which are connected to each other by roadways. One or more of them could well serve as the starting point for our lines, and we'd like your recommendations on that selection.

A second important issue is locating routes where the line would have to be above-ground, and where it could be in-ground. And, related to this, identifying any right of way clearances that will be required. Keep in mind, there are aboriginal land rights, lands reserved for existing and future mining operations, public parks, and timber and hydroelectric operations that will need to be taken into account in planning routes. Consider all of what I've outlined as phase one of your contract, and we're thinking of two years for completion. I trust you find that agreeable?"

Mel said, "Yes, indeed. We will need to deepen our understanding of this landmass, which as you said, is largely uninhabited and has no road systems. We have already determined that we will need a geologist to supplement what we already know from the available research of the area. We have a search underway to find a specialist in this field to join our staff, but in the interim I've been assured that an Instructor we will use from the University of Maine has all the skills necessary for this initial stage of the project. I should note that he referred to Quebec as a goldmine for the study of the Ice Age. His specialty is glacial geology."

"That makes good sense, Mel," Jon replied. "I've already contacted the appropriate officials from the Makivik Corporation[4] at their district offices here in Montreal and made arrangements for you to obtain the necessary travel and field study permits, and I will be visiting the Quebec Utilities Department in the next several days regarding permits for the lower region of the province."

Mel said, "We already know that Quebec is huge, but when we looked at the distances between the sites where we might collect grab-samples and record our observations, we had a new appreciation for just how huge it really is. I mean, I just learned that it's as far from here in Montreal to northern Nunavik as it is from here to Miami!"

Jon nodded his understanding and added, "The most effective way to get around will be by Air Inuit, operated by the Makivik Corporation out of Montreal as well as from Quebec City. They provide air service to all the coastal villages. And, we expect you will also be using local helicopter services in a couple of places to reach some inland sites. Keep in mind that eventually, if any line routes should come closer than five miles from any Inuit and Cree villages and their protected hunting and fishing grounds, we'll need to put together what is known as a Benefit and Impact Agreement. We'll get Makivik to help us with that."

"On that subject," Mel says, "I seem to recall news of the

4   Makivik, which in Inuktitut means "To Rise Up," is a fitting name for an organization mandated to protect the rights, interests and financial compensation provided by the 1975 James Bay and Northern Quebec Agreement, the first comprehensive Inuit land claim in Canada, and the more recent offshore Nunavik Inuit Land Claim Agreement that came into effect in 2008.
The Corporation's distinct mandates ranges from owning and operating large profitable business enterprises and generating jobs; to social economic development, improved housing conditions, to protection of the Inuit language and culture and the natural environment. Makivik's work demonstrates the extent that modern aboriginal treaties or land claim settlements could benefit governments and Inuit. (Source: https://jsis.washington.edu/canada/news/from-igloos-to-the-internet-inuit-in-the-21st-century/)

native Inuit and Cree residents of Quebec objecting to the whole idea of pipelines. And, later, when we look at lines from Quebec south through Maine to the coast at Portland, we'll have to get up to speed on where they might cross lands claimed by Native Americans—and I understand that is a hot issue at the moment."

"Yes," Jon said, "We will need to be sensitive to land claim issues not only here in Quebec, particularly in the northern area known as the Nunavik, but further to the north into the area now called Nunavut."

Mel answered, "Yes, I read something about that myself before coming up here." He and his colleagues were just beginning to learn about the history of right-of-way controversies and the ongoing struggles by developers to find most-direct pathways for their delivery system infrastructure.

The two men finished their meeting and were leaving the Inn when Mel spotted a man walking past the entrance, apparently heading to the University. He recognized him as a former student attending a seminar that Mel conducted for undergraduates at McGill.

"Roger?" Mel said, catching the man's attention. "Roger Gagnon?"

The man turned and recognized his former instructor. "Yes?" he answered. "That's me. You're Mel Johnson, aren't you. I remember you. I attended one of your seminars when I was a sophomore."

"Yes, you did. How are you? What are you up to these days?"

"I'm on my way to my office, and by the way, it's Dr. Roger Gagnon now. I supervise the geology lab over at the Center."

"Well, congratulations, Dr. Gagon. By that I'm presuming you are doing well."

"Yes, indeed. By the way, when will we see you back behind the podium, eh?"

"Not immediately, at least for me, but one of my colleagues, Eddy Burns, will be on board next term—for a couple of weeks. He's a busy man about to get even busier."

"That's good to hear. By the way, what are you doing here in town?"

"Our firm will be undertaking a study of potential pipeline

routing plans here in the Province, and I just finished a meeting with our employer, the Northpipe Corporation. How about you? What keeps you busy?"

"I spend most of my time with advanced degree candidates in the Geology Department, which means lots of hours on the microscope. And, by the way, you may remember that when I was an undergrad I had a summer job collecting ground samples on the 117 Highway north of Mt Laurier, my hometown."

"Yes, I remember you telling me about that. If I remember correctly, that, too, was part of a proposed pipeline route study. What did you learn from that work? Are the results available? It would save us some serious time if it could be shared."

"Interesting that you should ask," Dr. Gagnon responded with a smile.

———

I just love these new kayaks, thought the young Roger Gagnon. He was resting in his narrow yellow boat a short distance away from the beach where his friends were preparing for a last-of-the-day swim. All ten of them had just returned from paddling to a small island near the middle of Lac au Barges, which was a short drive east from the city of Mont-Laurier in Quebec Province. They had spent a few hours on the island, where they shared a lunch together sprawled around a small driftwood fire. He and his friends were all students at McGill University in Montreal, enjoying their first outing after completing their first year of studies.

A few hours later, Roger returned to Mt. Laurier where he would be spending the summer with his mother, Nicole, at the small, family-owned Bed and Breakfast known as Lit et Petit-Dejeuner. The B&B had been in operation for more than fifteen years, and was located a short distance from the better-known Gite Au Pied du Courant on the Rue du Portage on the northern shore of the Riviere du Lievre, a tributary of the Ottawa River. The river courses through the downtown area on its way to the Capitol and is a prominent feature of this French-speaking community.

A city of more than 13,000, Mt. Laurier is located roughly halfway between Montreal and Abitibi, almost 200 miles northwest of Montreal and nearly 300 miles southeast of the border with Ottawa south of James Bay.

With the death of her husband, Pierre, two years ago, Nicole was forced to sell their family home and soon after moved into the B&B, where she was working hard to strengthen its growing reputation as a first class hotel and dining establishment. Roger was assigned living space in a small former storage closet behind the kitchen, where he would spend his summers while attending McGill. He also did his best to help out with chores at the B&B and spend as much time with his maman as possible

Nicole had left a note in the kitchen saying that she was out shopping and would be returning late. She also left a serving of coq au vin for Roger to warm up for his evening meal, along with a reminder that he needed to be up early for his first day of work. He smiled broadly as he lapped up last of the delicious leftover and headed for his cot in the storage closet. He was asleep almost as soon as his head touched the pillow.

One of his classmates at McGill, the young, gorgeous, Ms. Lisette Alemaque swam to his kayak and pulled herself across the bow as Roger reveled in the sight of that shapely bikini-clad body about to share space on his small vessel. He held his double-bladed oar across his lap and leaned to one side to maintain balance, when ... clang! A horrendously loud noise wakened him from his dreams, at that moment filled with the memory of yesterday's outing on Lac au Barges.

Just as he recognized that the disturbance had come from the adjacent kitchen, Nicole stepped to the doorway and said, "Sorry, Roger. Didn't mean to wake you quite that way, eh. The pan slipped right out of my hands."

Roger said, wiping his eyes and grinning, "That's okay, maman. I do need to be up anyway."

Today was to be the first day of Roger's summer job, hired by a recruiting firm, which had interviewed him at the McGill campus the previous spring. He would be working for Line Surveys, Ltd., a Montreal-based company specializing in plotting potential routes for oil and natural gas pipelines. As such routes commonly shared established paths such as roadways and rail-beds, Roger's task was going to be collecting ground samples along Rte 117 between Mt Laurier and Rouyn Noranda, located 250 miles to the northwest approaching the border with Ottawa.

It was still dark outside as Roger and Nicole shared a breakfast of poached eggs and ham on toast topped off with café au lait and a thick slab of freshly baked banana bread. Soon after, with the first hint of sunrise, Roger headed west in a company pickup truck to join Rte 117, known locally as the Boule des Ruisseaux. He continued driving west until the nearby Mt Laurier Airport came into view.

Just shy of the airfield and north of Lac des Sources he pulled to the roadside and parked. Although traffic was light this time of day, and likely to remain so, he placed the required safety cones in front of and behind the vehicle. From the rear, he pulled two satchels. One contained his sampling tools, and the other a collection of small, aluminum tubes with blank labels.

His instructions were to collect a total of ten samples at each stop, five on each side of the road at fifty meter intervals, positioning each sample site twenty meters distant from the highway's centerline.

At the first site, 100 yards to the rear of his truck, Roger stepped of the required distance from the roadway's centerline and found a suitable spot. He first used a post-hole digger and made a small hole one meter deep. At the bottom of that hole, he inserted a core sampler, which he screwed another eight feet down into the earth. When he pulled the sampler back out, he had captured a 6" long core about 2" in diameter.

Using a special tool, he gently pushed the intact core sample into one of the aluminum tubes, assigned a number (#1 in this case) to the label, and recorded in his log the sample number, location in relation to a highway mile-marker, the date, and time.

He repeated the sampling at the remaining nine sites, at which point he returned to his truck. It had taken him almost two hours to finish his work at this first stop. The next site was 5 miles further west, so he figured it should be possible to get that work completed, stop someplace along the way for lunch, and then head back home. He knew that as he worked further away from Mt. Laurier at intervals of five miles, he would be spending more time traveling than sample collecting. Either he would have to get started much earlier each day, or figure out a plan for overnight stops.

It took until mid-August for Roger to complete his sampling work, gathering all 250 cores of earthly material and turning the core-sample collection and his logs over to his employers. He was told that the samples would be placed in storage in Montreal until the company could arrange for an analysis. Meanwhile, Roger was given a series of routine tasks to keep him occupied until he returned to classes for the fall term.

———————

"So, what did the analysis tell you?" Mel asked.

"Interestingly, the samples were never analyzed—at least at the time. It turns out the company that hired me was acquired early that fall, just as I was completing my work. The Ottawa-based company relocated and merged the Montreal operation with their headquarters near the Capitol in Ontario. Somehow, during the process of the acquisition, the samples in that Montreal storage locker were overlooked and have remained so until just recently.

The new owners discovered my logs and found out where the samples were stored. When they learned that I now work here at the Center's lab, they contacted me and asked that we do the analysis. That's pretty much what I've been doing now for the past month or so. Would you care to have a look at what I've discovered?"

"Most certainly," Mel replied. "I can make time right now. Let's go see."

After a short walk to the Earth and Planetary Science Center, Mel followed Roger to his lab and workshop, where the samples were laid out for analysis.

"I'm going to skip over the samples closest to Mt. Laurier, which were unremarkable—as are most of them. By the way, should you plan a route for an in-ground pipeline along Rte 117, you should have no problems in general. Should be easy digging. These next sets, however, are more interesting."

Roger pointed to a ten-core sample set arranged on his bench in a semi-circle.

"Take a look here," Roger said, identifying a particular core that had been sliced in half along its length. "What you're looking at is material known as undifferentiated glacial till. It looks like ordinary gravel, with small rocks, some clay, and sand. We know from other studies of this area that such material was transported some distance during the last advance of the ice shield. To answer the question of origin, we work backwards using as our guide indicators showing us the direction the ice flowed.

The problem is, till can be created and moved in one direction, then later as the ice shield repeatedly retreated and advanced, moved in an altogether different direction, or perhaps simply spread out in a new pattern—not unlike the delta region of a major river. Or, as we are now learning, picked up and transported far to the south, across the St. Lawrence, and deposited in Maine. In other words, tracking the stuff is a difficult challenge. And, to make it more confusing, there were at least twelve major ice shield advances.

Pointing to a large map of the Province, Roger said, "You will note that when we look up-ice, to our north, there are two likely locations: Lac Kaackawakamak and the Resevoir Gouin; and Resevoir Cabonga. Possibly coming into play are two other water bodies: Lac Baskatlong and Riverie Nottaway. We would typically point to these locations because they were most likely gouged into the then existing surface by the massive forces of the ice shield, creating enormous volumes of primary deposits. It is entirely possible for materials like this to be transported from such distances. We also compare our analysis of the materials with the parent rocks in that area."

"Do I sense you have some question about these locations as the source?" Mel said.

"Yes, as it so happens, I do, and mostly because of what we are finding in this sample and a few others. Among the minerals we found traces of chrome diopside, eclocite garnet, and cr-pyrobe minerals. Interestingly, it turns out these are diamond indicators.

"I'm not following you and your apparent uncertainty about the source."

"Well, this is what it could mean, and it's what I am tending to accept as the most plausible explanation." One of my students called them 'down ice diamonds.' She said they demonstrated the oldest proof of gravitation: everything runs downhill, even two-mile thick ice."

Roger returned to the map and pointed to the northeast, where he identified a large, round feature labeled as the Manicouagan Crater.

"We first have to exclude impact diamonds, so we look at impact sites." Pointing to the map again, Roger said, "From what we know about this crater, reputed to be the sixth largest on Earth at more than 60 miles in diameter, it was formed more than 200 million years ago by the impact of an asteroid or comet. From everything we know, in those times the Province was hammered by asteroids and meteorites, only some of which have been identified. The ones we do know about are widespread, from the Pingualuit in the far north to the Presqu'Ile and the Lle Rouleau not far away toward James and Hudson Bays.

There is even some evidence to suggest," Roger continued, "that Ungava Bay, itself, was created by a monster asteroid impact. And, you may have heard about the theory that when these cosmic bodies impact an area of the Earth's surface made up of high amounts of graphite and carbon they can instantly produce what are known as impact diamonds."

"I think I read that somewhere. Alright, so tell me," Mel responded. "What are the diamonds in these samples telling you?"

"Well, we look for primary sources: kimberlites. These diamondiferous materials we are looking at here are microscopic, and certainly not gemstones—the kind you'd find in jewelry stores. And, more importantly, we now know they are not impact diamonds. We happen to be located on some of the oldest known bedrock found anywhere in the world, known as the Superior orogen—or crust upwelling.

There is a major fault line, running across the Province roughly northeast to southwest, along which there are a number of minor faults that break off at roughly 90 degrees, southeasterly for the most part. It is along such faults that volcanoes are produced as the tectonic plates beneath them shift and work against each other."

"I think I see where you're going with this," Mel replied. "Volcanoes are what bring molten magma to the surface, and in many cases, leaving behind rock pipes known as kimberlites. Am I on the right track?"

"Yes, you are. And, as to the question of where these particular diamond indicators might have originated, we have to remember that during the final stages of the ice shield melt, water courses within, under, and on top of the ice carried off massive amounts of till. So, if we follow a trail to the northeast, to the Otish Mountains toward the border with Labrador, we find an equally likely source."

"So you are thinking of volcanic activity and kimberlites in that region?"

"Yes, and in fact, even further northeast, to the Ungava Bay region, where we kimberlitic activity is well documented. There is more work to be done before we can confirm the likely source, but right now we are concentrating our efforts on comparing the mineralogy of the till in the Mt Laurier area to parent sources in the Otish basin. We are also in touch with some geologists in Maine, because they are finding some of this same Quebec-based till in their eskers and moraines."

Visit to Kangiqsualujjuaq

The Nunavik Region of Northern Quebec

Some people are capable of sleeping most anywhere, even in a moving vehicle. Mel Johnson was not one of them, and in spite of having spent the better part of this early summertime day stuffed into an airplane, he has remained alert and observant for most of the 1,000 mile long journey with Air Inuit—except for this last leg, when he finally succumbs to fatigue. He has managed to nap for just over an hour when he is jarred awake as the plane drops into an unexpected pocket of rough air and his head slips off a pillow and collides with the rigid padding surrounding the window opening.

He sits up, quickly composes himself, and looks across the aisle to his young colleague and traveling companion, Dr. Mark DeLyon, an Instructor with the University of Maine's Geology Department. Mark appears comfortable enough, thoroughly engrossed in a book on the Nunavik history, and apparently is tolerating the jerking and bouncing like a veteran air traveler.

As soon as word spread among the teaching faculty about the project, just as the spring term was ending, Mark contacted Mel and asked to be considered for the assignment. Just 25 years old, Mark is a dark haired, athletically built young man from northern Maine with a BS degree from Boston University and PhD from the Cornell University. Mel was impressed with the young man's academic record and confident he would contribute to the work ahead.

They initially met in Marks office at the University of Maine, where they had access to a wide array of information on the geology of the Province of Quebec. Using a topographical map as a guide, and taking into account Jon Martin's comments, they began to construct an overall preliminary plan.

———

After marking two broad areas on the tip of the Ungava Peninsula, oriented east and west, Mel said, "It would appear that what I've called Area I. will be the primary location for the head of any future pipeline. The oil and gas reserves seem to be distributed east and west of Baffin Island, and a direct route from there to the pipeline would thus be the shortest. Until and unless additional reserves are found in Hudson Bay or to the northwest, in the interior island area, Area II, should be considered secondary for pipeline routing.

The next question is how to get from there to Quebec City. The primary route should avoid mountains, of course, and be run generally on as level ground as possible. So, I'm thinking the western area of the Province would be the most sensible starting point, staying well inland to avoid conflict with native hunting and fishing grounds."

———

It is late in the afternoon. This the second leg of the trip, which began in Montreal, has taken the two men northward through Schefferville, a small village on the border with Newfoundland and Labrador. They will soon be landing at Kuujjuaq, the largest of over a dozen Inuit villages in the Nunavik in northern Quebec Province.

The village itself is set against the western shore of the Koksoak River, some 50 miles inland (or upriver) along the southwestern shore of Ungava Bay. The nearby Torngat Mountain Range, straddling the border between northern Quebec and Newfoundland-Labrador about 125 miles to the east, will be the first of several areas Mel and Mark plan to visit. The plan is to make a brief ground-view assessment of several areas in Quebec—locations identified as potential sites for the transfer of oil and natural gas to pipelines.

The Inuit village of Kuujjuaq developed around the site of a WWII U.S. Army air station called Crystal I. The base was turned over to the Canadian Government at the end of the World War II. A number of religious and social service organizations established themselves there, and later, a local Inuit village known as Siamuk and a Hudson's Bay fur trading operation, long established on the opposite shore a short distance away, relocated to the base location and helped to expand its population to the present day level of over 2,500. Because of its excellent paved runways and adjacent support facilities, the village gained a reputation as an important transportation center. Siamuk subsequently adopted the name Kuujjuaq.

The village is also the headquarters for the Makivik Corporation. Representing the interests of the more than 9,000 Nunavimmiut in the Nunavik, or the northern section of Quebec Province, the Corporation evolved from the James Bay-Northern Quebec Agreement of 1975. Prior to this Agreement, most of those living in southern Quebec and other Provincial areas of Canada had little to no regard for the land rights and communal customs of the Amerindians who had populated this Arctic region for more than ten thousand years. There were many who continued to either reject outright or ignore the hard-won rights the native peoples had to the land and its many resources.

Mel peered outside. The large overhead wings of the plane provided an unobstructed view earthward, but the only thing he could see was the topmost layer of a cloud deck that seemed to go on forever in all directions, an image that had remained unchanged since beginning their journey just after dawn.

Their route was taking them toward a region where the Hudson Straits merge with the Labrador Sea, north and east of Quebec Province. Suddenly, there was a subtle shift in the pitch of the propellers as the pilot prepared for his initial descent. Mel watched as the cloud deck neared, and after several minutes of experiencing minor bounces and a few more serious bumps, sometimes followed by the plane actually shifting sideways, they were enshrouded by clouds and then there was nothing to see.

The bucking and shifting continued for almost ten more minutes until finally, the ground appeared more than 3,000 feet below and the ride smoothed. The landing on the long, paved runway a few minutes later was pleasantly smooth, and after a short taxi the plane came to stop at the terminal.

After checking in at the departure desk to confirm their reservations for the next leg of their trip north to Quaqtaq three days hence, the two men used a courtesy van to deliver their equipment and most of their belongings to the nearby Coop Hotel. Meanwhile, in daylight which lasts for more than 18 hours at this time of the year, and in seasonal temperatures in the high forties, Mel and Mark took the opportunity to stretch their legs and chose to walk to a nearby restaurant for their only real meal of the day.

"I didn't know salmon could taste so good," Mark said after finishing the last bite of the restaurant's featured favorite.

"What you just ate is actually known as arctic char, a close relative," Mel said. "You might not have noticed the menu read 'salmon, trout or char in season.'"

"It matters not," Mark replied. "I was so hungry they could have served me boiled shoe leather."

"When we get out in the field tomorrow," Mel said, "You'll see some of the absolute best rivers and streams and pools for catching these fish to be found anywhere in the world. People come here just for the fishing, so I'm told."

———————

With a good night's rest and anxious to get on with his first ground exploration, first thing the next morning they located the offices of a local outfitter, whose business included a set of seasonal camps on the eastern shore of Ungava Bay as well as access to a single-engine float plane and a helicopter. In this region of northern Quebec, there are no roads, and any equipment allowing visitors to get around quickly is in high demand.

The largely unpopulated region to the east of Ungava Bay is made up of a northward-pointing narrow peninsula, bisected by the Torngat Mountain range. Labrador's Torngat Mountains National Park straddles the border between northern Quebec and Newfoundland and Labrador. Most of the park's rugged, treeless land surface lies about 1,000 ft above sea level, cut through by deep Fjords. Its coastline is notable for its river systems rich with trout, salmon and char. Its highest mountains reach about the same elevation as Mt Katahdin in northern Maine—around 5,000 ft.

They were greeted at the Outfitter's office by a young Inuk staffer whose nametag read Tukkiapik. She informed them that she was a recent graduate of the local Jaanimmarik High School and that they should please call her Trish. The file containing their travel arrangements and land access permission requests was quickly located, having been forwarded weeks earlier from Mel's Marblehead office.

"Good morning, gentlemen," she greeted, scanning the file contents. "I see you're planning for a two-day stay at the Camp and plan to visit the Fjord area of the Torngats. I have your access requests here."

Mel said, "That's correct, Trish, or Ms. Tuk-kya-pick. I apologize if I'm not pronouncing that correctly."

"No mind. You're as close as you need to be," their host replied with a grin, followed quickly by a shy smile aimed mostly at young Mark.

Mel continued, "We'll be making photographs of land features and collecting a few small surface samples of some of the local rocks, which we'll send to a lab in the U.S. for analysis. We will also be recording our location at all times with equipment we'll be carrying."

"Will you be armed?" Trish asked.

"We will only be carrying small knives. No weapons, if that's what you are asking."

"Well, please be advised that it's mandatory for you to have an armed guide along, which I'll be happy to arrange. Your guide, who happens to be my brother, will meet you at the Camp where you'll be staying, out on the Bay. That area is well-known bear habitat—the brown type as well as the polar bear. This is for your own protection."

"I did read something about that in your website, now that I think about it," Mark said, quietly and slightly embarrassed at the oversight.

"Yes, the fish are plentiful out there, and the bear are always hungry. It's good to keep that in mind," Trish explained, smiling at the display of apparent naivety.

"I have your tickets here for your trip to Kangiqsualujjuaq across the Bay. It's about an hour's flying time away. There you'll be met and flown on by floatplane to the Camp, about one half-hour more further on. Then, as you have requested, we can get you to the Fjord area by helicopter from the camp, weather permitting. It should be fine for the next several days, so you ought to be able to get your work done as planned without incident. By the way, if you wish to enter the Park's grounds, there will be people at the camp who can assist. Some of the Park's land is in Quebec, and some is in Labrador and Newfoundland. It is in Inuit territory called Nunatsiavut. Do you have any further questions for me?"

"Not at the moment," Mel replied. "And thank you for your help. We have a full set of maps, which we'll be using. All that's left now is to get our things and head for the airport. I'm hoping to see you when we return. We'll need your help with ground arrangements at our next stop in Quaqtaq. "

Seated at the air terminal in Kuujjuaq waiting for their hour-long flight to Kangiqsualujjuaq, Mel said to Mark, "Have you had time to do any advanced study of the geology in this area?"

"Yes, I have," Mark replied, not wanting to appear totally ignorant but also hoping not to come across as overconfident with his limited knowledge of this little-traveled area of the world. "I read a report out of the University of Ottawa that pointed to this area as supported by some of the oldest rocks known to man. If memory serves, we are on the Archean craton of the Superior Province, which runs back across the Great Lakes area and on down into the central states. More specifically, we are now on the Southeastern Churchill Section of the Superior.

In addition to being buried under a two mile thick layer of ice, which cycled back and forth at least a dozen times over uncounted centuries and reshaped the entire surface, a good deal of the formative landmass here in Quebec still shows pre-ice age evidence of having been pounded by asteroids and meteorites and all sorts of other cosmic objects. A lot of them left their mark as impact craters, which are not difficult to find on land, but because of their remoteness, difficult to reach. Several more have been identified in recent times through satellite photography and aeromagnetic mapping.

And, you may also have read, there is evidence of a structural fault here that runs roughly from this area–Ungava Bay, southwest across Quebec to an area near James Bay, north of the Great Lakes region. And there is evidence of structural zones all along that line, across the southern sections of the Province. It is along these fault lines that a great deal of uplifting occurred, bringing with it magmatic materials—some of which, by the way, is diamondiferous."

"Interesting you mention that," Mel said, "You know, I had a meeting a while ago with a friend at McGill's Earth and Planetary Science Center, and he, too, is finding the same thing in ground samples collected from the Mt Laurier area. But remember, it isn't diamonds we're after: it's about finding a way and the best routing for moving the oil and natural gas that the Canadian government predicts is hiding under all this ice and snow and rock up out of the ground, into a pipeline, and down to the St. Lawrence–and eventually all the way to Portland, Maine."

Visit to Quataq

Nunavik, Quebec

Mel and Mark finished their two days of trekking around part of the eastern shore of Ungava Bay, collecting several dozen rock samples, taking hundreds of photographs, mapping locations, and conducting preliminary tests of the permafrost. They agreed that the area with its deep and dark fjords, waterfalls gracing the rocky sides of steep rock faces, gigantic twice-daily tidal flows, and swiftly moving rivers filled with an wide assortment of fish and other marine animals, was unlike anything they had ever seen. They were awestruck by the wild scenery and ruggedness that surrounded them each day.

They also concluded that any pipelines in this area would have to be built above ground, and that meant that great care would have to be given to its impact on local wildlife. They returned to Kuujjuaq, finalized arrangements for their trip to Quaqtaq with Ms. Tukkiapik. After a good night's sleep at the Coop Hotel, they are now flying north on Air Inuit.

Based on his study of the geology of northern Quebec and some hurried study of land maps prior to leaving his home in Maine several days earlier, Mark knew the peninsular of land they were approaching was shaped like a right-handed woolen mitten, palm down, with the tip of the thumb projecting into a small inlet off the Hudson Strait to the west called Diana Bay, or Tuvaaluk in Inuktitut language. The Strait itself and passage to Hudson Bay was further to the north—above the fingertips, with Ungava Bay to the east—adjoining the little finger. Further to the east, Ungava Bay opened to the Sea of Labrador and the Atlantic beyond.

Jon Martin had targeted the locale as one possible starting point for a pipeline, noting that hydroponic testing in the Straits and the nearby Diana Bay had already shown promise as a source of natural gas. Further tests for oil were planned but not yet approved, given the continuing dispute as to who was to have rightful control of the seabed under the ice.

Both Mel and Mark had divided the time since leaving Kuujjuaq between reading and glancing at the barren landscape. From the right side seat, Mel said, "What do you know about that island out there in the Bay?"

Mark, in the opposite seat, replied, "It's called Akpatok. It's shaped like a giant birthday cake, something like 30 miles long and about half as wide. All limestone and probably wicked tough on shoe leather. Most of the year it's locked in by sea ice and takes on the look of an iceberg on steroids. Notice that it's mostly flat on top?"

Reading from a recent copy of a Canadian Geographic Magazine he had picked up while waiting at the terminal, he read, "'The rugged sides are near vertical, anywhere from 300 to 500 feet high, and buffeted daily by 40 foot tides. The island's sparse shoreline is summer home for the polar bear and walrus; a major nesting ground for the thick-billed Murres; and the island is visited by the occasional fox, caribou and wolf. The Inuit consider it a favorite hunting ground.'" Sometime, years ago, an oil company did some test drilling on one of the few landing spots. It doesn't say anything about what they may have learned.

Mel smiled and for the next few minutes absorbed what he had just learned from his traveling companion. Moments later, he remembered something about that island he learned before the meeting with Jon Martin.

"That island, and almost all the islands on Quebec's coastline, if I understand it correctly, will become part of the Nunavut. The

Nunavut will have its own government, located in the village of Iqaluit on Baffin Island, and that means we will soon have to figure out just who to work with to clear any pipeline routes. Here in the Nunavik, that's clear, but the recovery of oil or natural gas off the coast—from under the ice, most of the year, may occur in areas controlled not by this Province."

"So, looks like you'll be making some more arctic trips," Mark said.

"I imagine so," Mel replied. "But, back to the present. This place we're going to is one of the smaller villages, with a little over 200 permanent residents. The Makivik Corporation provided the names of Mayor, the City Manager, and the Chief of Police. They suggested we check in with them before we do any work, but they sent word ahead that we were coming. I have no idea how their names are pronounced. Hope we don't embarrass ourselves."

While the approach to Kuujjuaq a few days earlier was made above and then through a solid cloud deck, the sky this morning was clear and the view nearly unlimited. The shifting sound from the plane's engines signaled the start of their straight-in approach to the Quaqtaq airport. Their route was taking them over a range of small mountains, and another low range could be seen far ahead. The view east to Ungava Bay soon disappeared, replaced by the now dominant view of Diana Bay to the West.

———

After settling into the Coop Hotel near the center of the village, and enjoying a good night's rest, Mel and Mark's first stop was the Mayor's office, where they learned Mayor Annahatak was out of town dealing with a family emergency. They also learned that Police Chief Jaaka had accompanied the Mayor. That meant that two of the three people they were to meet were unavailable. In an adjoining building, they located City Manager John Ekomiak, and were given a warm greeting. He was an older man, perhaps as old as 70 — although it was difficult to say, and was neatly dressed in blue jeans and a plaid shirt.

"Come on in," Ekomiak said. "We received word from Kuujjuaq that you would be coming. Welcome to you both. My name is John. How might we here in Quaqtaq be of help? "

"Thank you, sir," Mel replied, as he and Mark seated themselves in front of the City Manager's desk. "My name is Mel Johnson and my companion here is Mark DeLyon. We expect we'll be here only a few days, and I'll be happy to share our work schedule, but why don't you first begin by telling us about yourself and the people of your village," Mel suggested.

Before answering, John stepped to a small counter in the corner of his office on which sat a gas burner, a steaming teakettle, and an assortment of mugs. He offered tea to his guests, both of whom nodded 'yes, please,' and returned with three mugs of hot water. A small, brightly colored tin containing several types of tea sat on his desk, and after opening it, he offered Mel and Mark their choice of tea bags. He also offered sugar, but both men declined.

Then, easing back in his chair, the elder man said, "Well, I was born and raised in this area. My family lived a nomadic life when I was a child, traveling with other families by dog sled to winter quarters on the offshore islands and then back and forth between here and the village of Kuujjuaq, a place you just visited.

When we were teenagers, my family was forced to send my sister and I south to live with relatives in a small village near Schefferville. We both went to a residential school there, and I went on to attend college in Montreal. It was during that time things really changed here in the north—when the James Bay land claims Agreement was adopted. You know about that, I presume?"

"Yes, we do," Mel answered.

"Shortly afterward, the village you see today was created, and people from the Government and the Province began to visit and helped to bring things like housing, a health clinic, a general store, and of course a school. And we now have our own airport, with weekly flights when the weather permits. All that has taken a lot of getting used to, because it is so different from our traditional way of life.

In college I studied history and government, although my friends constantly remind me we would be better off if I had studied mechanics. You see, we spend a good amount of time every day keeping our machines in working order, from outboard engines to snowmobiles to generators. While the days of long distance travel by dog sled are almost a thing of the past, some in the village still think life was better then.

I rejoined my family here and now I've reached an age where I am no longer able to make long trips over land to winter hunting grounds, or to spend days on the ice waiting for a fat seal to appear at a breathing hole. So, I keep myself busy doing what I can to keep our small village—we are just over 220 people now, operating as smoothly as I can. We oversee things like road maintenance, city services, and building construction. I expect you will want to visit Mayor Annahatak as well as Chief Jaaka, but I believe they were called out of town."

"Yes, we found that out," Mel replied. "We'll try them tomorrow, perhaps, if they've returned."

"Now, about your plans for this visit."

"First, thank you for taking time to meet with us. We are here representing a private firm called Northpipe Corporation. The assignment that Mark and I have been given is to re-examine the known topography and the landforms in this general area. As you know, tests were conducted in and around the Bay and further out into the Straits to determine whether or not it might be a source of natural gas. We understand that some of those initial tests generated positive results. We also understand that testing for oil remains to be done." *As soon as someone figures out who actually controls the land under the ice, he thought.*

"If sometime in the future the recovery of such resources were to be proven feasible and commercially viable, the oil and gas would have to be transported south to refineries and processing facilities in and around Quebec City. How far into the future this might all happen is an unknown, but the thinking is it will occur in a decade or so.

A more direct transfer to the refineries would be by pipeline, since shipping would be limited to a few months in the summer. Our task is to examine the projected routing such pipelines would take, and either confirm the viability of those routes or suggest alternatives. Incidentally, from what we've been shown, none of the proposed routes would cross the land of this village. In fact, none would come close to the five-mile limit. I understand that is important to you and all the others of this community."

Ekomiak took a few minutes to absorb what he had just been told, appearing to be calm and relaxed as he mulled over the information Mel had given him. Mel, however, could see that the City Manager was anything but calm and relaxed. His hands were resting on the arms of his chair, but he was absently clenching and unclenching them as he prepared to respond.

"First, I want to thank you for your frankness and for sharing this information," John said, after a pause to take a deep breath. "We are fully aware of the testing that was done for natural gas. For us, such developments come with a mixed blessing. On the one hand, pipelines could mean more jobs for our people and other improvements to our village. At the same time, we are concerned about the impact it will have on our wildlife and our more traditional way of life.

I'll give you an example. You see, tests for oil and gas deposits require the use of a large ship to drag an underwater noise generator that sets off loud explosions—which was done all up and down the Straits between here and Baffin Island. We did what we could at the time to stop it, but our efforts were denied by the Justices of the Crown's court. As you might suppose, the basis of our plea centered on the protection of our lands and our wildlife.

The counterargument, that there is no factual evidence that such testing threatens the fish, narwhale, beluga, and seals that our people use for food and have survived on for centuries, won the day. All we were told is that such testing was in full compliance with the terms of the James Bay Agreement, and I and our other village elders have been assured by the leaders of the Makivik Corporation that any further testing—such as for oil, for example, will comply as well.

If you were to ask me—or any of us here, if we are in favor such work, or if we like it, then I, too, will be equally frank and tell you the answer is no. By the way, I presume you are familiar with the details of the James Bay pact?"

That's the second time he's brought that up, Mel thought. "Yes, we are, but by your comments just now, I gather you aren't all that pleased with it."

"If you will indulge me, I'd like to tell you a little story," John replied. "We Intuits have lived in the Nunavik—that's what we and others now call this northern part of the Province, for a very long time. We came from as far away as Greenland to the east and Alaska and northern Siberia to the west and as far back as twelve thousand years ago. That was not long after the end of the last ice age.

This has always been our world, which we call our Nunangat-meaning the land, water and ice. We are survivors. We adapt to conditions as we find them and learn how to survive on the natural and renewable resources available to us. We never claimed to 'own' this land or the seas surrounding us. But we took care of it. We made sure to protect the things that sustained us. And then the white man arrived. If this is beginning to sound familiar—like the history of your own Native American Nations and Tribes, then perhaps you will appreciate what I'm telling you.

The white man, first from Europe and later from nations to our south and from our west, brought disease and reduced our numbers. Then he began taking our whales and our fish and our animals for their fur and meat. Then he dammed our rivers to make electric power, ruining vast areas of our hunting and fishing grounds. In those early times, and I suspect you know the story, he forced us to send our children to far away residential schools. I, myself, was caught up in that practice. That proved to be a disaster, and the Crown and Provincial governments are still apologizing for that policy and doing what they can to right that wrong.

Then he discovered our Nunangat is rich in other things such as iron and nonferrous ores, gold, lead, zinc, copper, nickel, precious metals and diamonds. More recently, it is suggested that we may be sitting on a fifth of the world's petroleum and natural gas reserves.

Finally, while forcing us to change our traditional ways and end our nomadic way of life, the Crown and Provincial governments laid claim to our lands and reduced us to becoming dependent on them. We now live sedentary lives in small villages, learning new languages, eating different foods, requiring us to pay dearly for things we don't always understand with money that most of us have too little of.

There are some who believe that we are better off integrated— that's the term used, into the larger Canadian and Provincial societies, and that we should all somehow share in the Nunavik's natural wealth and riches—particularly those that are non-renewable. At the same time, this has left us living a life much like many of your own Native Americans have—on reservations. We here in Canada, too, have our own history of forcing the First Nation people onto reservations."

And I should add," he continued, "like many of those who live on reservations in your nation, we are doing our best to preserve and pass on to our children our traditional languages and customs.

After what you have just been told, you must think I am a just an old cynic, happy to see us return to our traditional nomadic ways," the City Manager replied. "But I am also a realist, and as one of those responsible for the welfare of this community, I have come to accept that we must now move forward—think forward, be more pragmatic about things, find different and better ways to adapt — just as we have always done."

"Well, thank you, sir, for your time, and for sharing your thoughts. You've given us much to think about," Mel said, somewhat overwhelmed by what he had just learned. He was also pleased to notice that Mark, too, had held his tongue, perhaps equally chastened.

Both men were thinking, I understand now why we might not always be greeted with open arms.

After two days of ground sampling, and making notations on their map for feasible locations for storage facilities and pipeline pumping stations—all of which were to the south of the village along the Diana Bay shoreline, Mel and Mark were satisfied that they had accomplished their assignment.

News From Back Home

Madison, Wisconsin

It is dark, a good hour before sunrise when Aunt Ellie arose early, as usual, dressed in her work clothes, and headed for the barn to feed her beef cattle. All signs pointed to another good day of early summer weather. She stepped through the barn's wide front door and, to her surprise found her niece Marie dragging a bale of hay along the central feed aisle.

"You're up early," Aunt Ellie said, catching Marie somewhat by surprise.

"Oh, Aunt Ellie," Marie replied. "Good morning. Yes, I fell asleep at my desk, finally getting near the end of all that homework I was assigned by the Law School, and when I did wake up, I discovered it was time to get to work."

"So, have you made a decision yet?"

"Not yet. I have a few questions about where I might have to go and how long I'd be there, and then there's Charlie. I'll want to discuss any assignment with him before I make a final decision. I'll have to work out how he'll be cared for, how often I can return for visits, and how to continue his schooling."

"For goodness sakes, Marie, you know he can stay here with me. He likes it here, and he is certainly doing well in school."

"Yes, he is. I suppose it might be wrong to take him out of school and away from his friends."

By mid-morning, Marie and her Aunt Ellie had finished their chores and were enjoying their breakfast at a small table in the kitchen. Charlie was up, settled on a sofa across the room near the front window. He was deeply engrossed in reading the latest issue of the National Geographic magazine when he spotted the mailman's car pulling up to their mailbox.

"I'll go get the mail," he volunteered, and dashed outside.

When he returned, he dropped the small stack of mail on the kitchen counter and handed one item to his mother, along with, "Hey, Mom, you got a package from Maine."

Marie looked at the large, manila envelope, sent from a law firm named Eames, Wilson, and Byers, whose return address read Jonesburg, Maine—a town just a short distance away from the village of Moreville, her old home town. Jonesburg is also the Piscataquis County Seat.

"Well, open it, Mom," Charlie said, as curious as anyone to learn what was inside.

"Ok, Ok," Marie answered, reaching for a letter opener. "Let's see what we have here."

Inside, she found a stack of a dozen or so documents along with a cover letter from the law firm. I guess I'll read the cover letter first, then we'll all know," she said. Sitting on a stool at the counter, she read aloud the following:

Eames, Brown & Gerrish

Attorneys at Law

Danielson, Maine 04468

Tel: 207-966-5000

Fax: 207-966-5940

Dear Ms. Webber,

We are forwarding the enclosed to the address obtained from the papers (see attached) of the late John Webber, of Moreville Maine. Records indicate said John Webber is your great-uncle.

John Webber is the registered title-holder of a certain parcel of land, located on Pleasant Street in the town of Moreville, consisting of some forty five acres of undeveloped land, three acres of developed land, on which are two habitable and six uninhabitable structures (see attached). To the best of our knowledge, all habitable structures are unoccupied.

There are no known liens on the property or any other assets of John Webber, and you should know that the present (market) valuation of the property (land and buildings) is in the order of $200,000. As of this writing, all local, county and state tax obligations are paid in full.

Our firm received a copy of the living will of one John Webber approximately one year ago, in which, upon his death, he requested the execution of a transfer-on-death deed, or beneficiary deed, granting you, Marie Webber, full title and all rights to said property.

The threshold of 120 days following John Webber's death now having been reached, we stand ready to complete said execution of this TOD deed with the County's Registrar of Deeds.

As the sole beneficiary, your presence will be required to complete this matter. Please contact our offices (see our telephone and fax number on the letterhead above) as soon as possible to arrange for an appointment.

Sincerely yours,

M. Eames

Maxwell Eames, Senior Partner

———

"Whew! I'm glad I'm sitting down," Marie said. "I didn't see this coming."

"Well for goodness sakes, it looks like old Johnny had a favorite grand-niece after all," Aunt Ellie replied with a smile.

"Does this mean we might be going to Maine?" Charlie asked.

"Maybe so, maybe so," Marie replied, turning to the remaining documents.

Visit to Akulivik

Northern, Quebec

Mel and Mark had spent two days, repeating in Quaqtaq more or less what they had done during their previous stop at Kuujjuaq: collecting rock samples, testing the permafrost, marking maps, and taking several dozens of photographs. They traveled across the peninsula to the Ungava Bay coast on all-terrain vehicles driven by local guides, and then explored a good portion of the Diana Bay's shoreline north and south of the village.

"Any pipelines out of this area will have to be above ground," Mark said, "just like those in Alaska."

"I agree, and I'll have to get John Jenkins started on it. He'll know how it should be done. I'll call him as soon as we get back home."

The Mayor and Police Chief still had not returned, so they were unable to meet them before it was time to depart for their next stop–more than 300 miles due west, to the Hudson Bay coast and the village of Akulivik. They departed early in the morning from Quaqtaq on Air Inuit and settled in for the two-hour trip across the Nunavik.

In a straight line, the trip would normally cover about 300 miles of uninhabited land, but as the two men were that's flight only passengers, the pilot had agreed to Mark's request to add a few miles to the trip by flying slightly more to the north and then follow the Illukotat River all the way to the village of Akulivik.

––––––––––

Fortunately, the skies were clear and the view of the ground was excellent. Several minutes into the flight, the pilot announced that the Pingualuit Crater was coming into view out the right side windows.

––––––––––

"That's what I wanted you to see," Mark said, as the clearly seen crater came into view. "It's one of many in this area, and very close to what is being called the Smith Belt—just to the north. That Belt, which more or less ranges across the Province from Ungava Bay to Hudson Bay, is being mined for nickel. There is also some copper, but from what I read, it may not be commercially viable right now to mine for it. The operators of the nickel mine built a road from the mine north to Deception Bay on the Straits, where the ore is hauled and then shipped out to Quebec City and on for processing in Ontario. Incidentally, that's the only road of any consequence north of the 55th parallel."

"As I recall, nickel originates from meteor impacts," Mel replied. "And you've already talked about this Province being slammed from one end to the other. So, this Pingualuit crater we are looking at, it must have occurred around the same time?"

"Most likely, and from what I understand, the crater's rim was much higher at one time, but now, after surviving at least two ice age advances, it has been reduced nearly to ground level. The lake it contains is some of the purest fresh water to be found anywhere, and it is one of the deepest anywhere on earth at more than 1,300 feet."

"Interesting," Mel said. "It looks almost perfectly round, doesn't it?"

"It is," Mark answered. "Back in the day, it was a commonly used landmark by military pilots."

The pilot announced over the speakers, "We're about to cross the headwaters of the Illukotat river. We'll follow it all the way in to Akulivik. Weather's good, so sit back and enjoy the ride. Unfortunately, there's not a lot to see up here—except, of course, for the odd musk ox herd, or maybe a flock of a million or so snow geese."

Mel and Mark were met at the Akulivik airport by Joe Agloolik, who introduced himself as manager of the local Coop Hotel. After loading their bags into the back of the hotel's four-door pickup truck, Joe drove them to the small village.

"Before we go to the Hotel, I'd like to show you our village," he said. After passing a number of homes and an assortment of variously sized support buildings, they arrived at a point of land that opened onto a wide view of Hudson Bay and the passage between the village and Smith Island.

"This land was where our people settled for the summer hunt. These waters are rich in seal and walrus. And the bays to our north and south are also favorite whale feeding grounds. Arctic char migrate each year through this passage, and we catch a lot of them."

"I had char recently," Mark interjected. "I now know why you like them so much."

"Well, we do, but not quite as much as a good slice of raw Beluga liver, or some smoked caribou tongue," Joe replied with a wide grin.

"I haven't had the pleasure … yet," Mark responded, also grinning. *Neither have I*, Mel thought, pretty sure he might not ever want to.

"Anyway, you should know that we are also within yards of the border with the new Nunavut territory. It runs down the center of the passage in front of us, meaning that Smith Island out there—and almost all other islands in Hudson Bay and the Straits and Ungava Bay, are about to come under the control of the Nunavut Government.

We have always used this land as a summer hunting camp, and then Hudson's Bay Traders set up a post nearby. Unfortunately, they also brought disease, and all but wiped us out. Then, those few left moved away, until the James Bay Agreement was adopted and a group of us decided to return to the land given us for a village. There are just over 600 of us here now."

The weather, which had been excellent for their arrival, but when Mel and Mark stepped outside the next morning, the sun had disappeared. There was a light mist drifting down through a thick blanket of fog, and it was considerably cooler than anything they had so far experienced.

Two young men appeared on all-terrain vehicles, quickly explaining that Joe from the Coop had instructed them to take Mel and Mark wherever they needed to go for the next two days. They were twins, named Robert and John Tiguaq, adopted sons of Joe and his wife. They were working at the Coop for the summer, helping with chores at the lodge and serving as guides to visiting fishing and hunting parties.

"I see you're wearing a red cap, John, and you, Robert, have a blue one. That right?" Mel said, amused and also admittedly guessing. *These guys are absolutely identical*, he thought.

"No, sir. Just the opposite," Robert replied, grinning widely. "Think red for Robert."

"Got it. So, can you get us north, along the shoreline, to the River outlet? We'll start there, and work our way in a wide circle around the village, about 10 miles out. That sound doable?"

"Yes, sir. Be prepared to get muddy, though. And you'd better wear these goggles," he added, handing both Mel and Mark a well-worn set with oversized yellow lens.

That turned out to be an understatement, and by the time they finished their survey two days later, collecting their grab samples, and loading their digital cameras with several dozens of photographs, all four of them returned the Coop coated in a thick layer of dried mud.

When Joe greeted them, he laughed and said, "If I didn't know my sons were driving, I couldn't tell one of you from the other."

That evening, after a hot shower and lots of clean-up work, they shared a most enjoyable dinner with the Agloolik family at the Coop, relating their experiences in the Nunavik and explaining that it would likely be several years before anyone would see a pipeline in the area, if ever. Much depended, of course, on whether proven reserves could be found and whether or not it would be feasible and economical to develop them.

They received, in return, much the same story they had heard earlier from John Ekomiak, City Manager of Kuujjuaq.

The next morning, with the weather now improving, they left Akulivik and returned to Montreal. Mark continued on to his home in Maine near the University in Orono, and Mel flew to Boston, where MOM met him up and drove him to his office in nearby Marblehead.

Mel sent word to his team that they were to gather in Marblehead in three weeks to review their preliminary findings and organize the work on their report to Northpipe, which would be submitted by the deadline, three months away. A week later, a package arrived from Mark, containing a report on the ground samples and his analysis of ground conditions from those areas he and Mel had visited.

Offices of DeWault Realty

The Village of Moreville, Maine

Arriving at Bangor's International Airport, Marie and Charlie selected a small rental car and together drove the seventy miles north to Moreville. As they entered the village, Marie immediately recognized several of the village's landmarks, including a former spool mill, and near the center of the main street, the post office and bank. She headed for the Driller House, the town's only hotel located behind and above the row of stores along the main street, where they had reservations.

They unpacked their few things, late in the afternoon, and both she and Charlie were hungry. Marie inquired about local restaurants and found that one, which she remembered, was still in open for business. Along the way to the restaurant, they passed by DeWalt Realty.

"That's where we're going in the morning, Charlie," Marie said, pointing to the sign in front of a small office building.

"I remember about that name," the boy replied. "You said you knew them when you lived here."

"Yes, I did. There was a DeWalt in the class behind me in school."

I haven't seen one person I recognize, and this town is showing more signs than ever that time is passing it by. I don't remember ever seeing so many run-down buildings. Makes me wonder how people get by, Marie mused as she and her son approached the restaurant.

Settling in at the Mama Kenniston's Café located next to the local golf course, Marie and Charlie quietly enjoyed a surprisingly delicious home-cooked dinner.

"What'd you do when you were here?" Charlie asked.

"What do you mean?" Marie replied.

"I mean, did you play sports, you know, or go to the movies? Stuff like that."

"No, Charlie, I didn't. Our family included a bunch of youngsters—nieces and nephews, and I spent most of my spare time tending them. We didn't have a lot of money, either, and besides, there wasn't much to do in town. This is a pretty small town, and there were just over a hundred kids in the entire high school. Many of my classmates lived on farms, or way outside town, so we didn't spend time doing things that a lot of other kids do."

———————

The next morning, Marie and Charlie drove to the office of the principal owner of DeWalt Realty, who had taken over the business from her parents five years earlier. Nancy DeWalt was close in age to Marie's mother, and as expected in any small town, she knew the story of Marie's disappearance a decade earlier. She was also a polite lady, and courteous enough to avoid any mention of it.

"You say you have no interest in continued ownership of the property, Marie," Nancy DeWalt said. "If that's the case, we would be happy to broker a sale. As it happens, we have two or three clients who have told us of their interest in that land. We know it fairly well because we recently managed the sale of a property a short distance away on that same street. Would you be willing to give us an exclusive on the sale?"

"Yes, indeed, and the sooner you can sell it, the better," Marie answered, curious as to how in the world this small town Realtor would be able to find buyers in this remote region.

"The portion of your land bordering the river, is a well-known sand and gravel ridge, and the rest of the acreage should contain ample timber assets to make it attractive. The roadside portion, some of which is cleared, can be easily be re-zoned for commercial development. Snowmobiling is growing in popularity, and there's a Canadian outfit that's already contacted us, looking for a location to open a new dealership. That site would be attractive to them. The old rail bed on the east side of the river is one of the most heavily used trails in the winter. The remaining buildings near the road appear to be beyond repair and would likely be demolished."

"That sounds fine to me, Nancy. My son and I drove by earlier this morning, and to be honest, I left that place several years ago and have no interest in keeping it."

"I understand," DeWalt replied, recalling the story of Marie's disappearance a decade earlier. "Although they've been vacant for quite some time, you might want to at least check through the buildings to make sure there isn't anything worth salvaging before we post our For Sale sign. In fact, if you don't mind, I'll go with you and give you a hand."

"What about keys? How are we going to get inside?"

"That's not a problem. I'll show you when we get there."

———————

Marie, Nancy and Charlie stood quietly in the yard of the Webber property, looking at a dilapidated doublewide trailer, two small, windowless houses that are partially collapsed, and three small tarpaper sheds with lean-to structures attached.

"Let's take a quick look through that big trailer first," Nancy suggested. "The door is broken on the rear side. If there's anything of value, it would be in there. I've peeked inside those other old shacks, and they are all but empty."

"That 'shack' on the left, the one with the chopping block in front, was once my home. I grew up there, with my mother," Marie says, her voice shaking slightly. "Whew. I haven't thought of the place in years. I'm almost ashamed to admit it, but now that I see it again, I wonder how we managed."

Nancy started to reply but instantly chose not to: she recognized she has nothing useful to say.

"Can I look in those sheds?" Charlie asked, changing the subject and pointing to the three smallest structures.

"Sure," Marie answered, "but be very careful, and let me know if you see anything worth keeping."

"Ok." Charlie dashed off as Marie and Nancy headed for the trailer.

Ten minutes later, after Marie and Nancy finished checking the bedroom, bathroom, closets, and cupboards, it was clear that the doublewide was littered with nothing but junk.

"It smells in here," Marie said. "Yeah, I agree with you, Nancy. This thing should be demolished. No one would ever want to live in it." Yeah, but then old Johnny did, she thought.

As the two women step back outside, they could see Charlie coming out of one of the sheds carrying a potato sack.

"What do you have there?" Marie asked, walking toward her son.

"Found it under some boards. There's a basket inside, or at least most of one. And inside the basket I found some pieces of glass, or something. Here, take a look," Charlie said, opening the sack and pulling out what looked like the retina of a creel.

"That's a Penobscot fishing creel," Nancy said after looking at the woven wood basket, "and it's pretty old. My husband has a new one almost like it. Same weave. He got it down in Old Town at the Reservation store."

Marie picked out two of the larger pieces from the creel and thought: *this isn't glass ... it's some kind of stone.* She held it up and her son Charlie noticed that as the sunlight passed through it made colors like a rainbow.

Two days later, having decided to extend her stay in Maine for a few days, Marie and Charlie made a side trip the campus of the

University of Maine in Orono to find out more about the stones.

———————

Mark DeLyon, engrossed in a microscopic examination of a marine clay sample recently collected from a gravel pit in the Kennebec River region of south central Maine by one of his students, missed the first intercom message: *Dr. DeLyon, Dr. DeLyon, please report to the first floor reception area.*

Only when it was repeated minutes later, did it register: Dr. DeLyon, please report to the first floor reception area.

Oh, he thought, *that's me!*

Foregoing the building's elevator, he left the lab bench and walked quickly to a nearby stairway and hustled down a flight of stairs, arriving a short distance away from the main entrance lobby and the building's reception desk. Waiting at the desk were two people: a tall, attractive woman dressed in jeans, lightweight blouse, sneakers and leather jacket; and a young boy, which he took to be her son, also wearing jeans, T-shirt, sneakers and dark windbreaker jacket.

"Oh, there you are," the receptionist called out when she saw him emerge from the stairwell. "Dr. DeLyon, this lady and her son need some help, and I thought you might be able to be of assistance. I hope we're not interrupting ..."

"No, that's alright. I was just doing some lab work." Turning to the two visitors and inviting them both to join him at an adjoining seating area, he said, "Good morning. I'm Mark DeLyon. I'm a Glacial Geologist here at the University. How might I help you?"

"My name is Marie Webber and this is my son, Charlie," she began. "We live in Wisconsin, but I originally came from a small town not far north of here. Moreville. Perhaps you know of it?"

"Yes. I'm quite familiar with that area."

"Well, I left there more than a decade ago, and now I'm back because one of my relatives died and left me with the title to some property. I've arranged for its sale, because I have no interest in retaining it. On a visit a few days ago with the Realtor who's handling the sale, we were checking what few buildings remain and my son came across something that we both found curious."

She withdrew a small bundle from her leather handbag and handed it to DeLyon. He opened the package to reveal the remains of a very old fishing creel. "Is this what you found? What made you curious?"

"Yes, and no. We learned from the Realtor that this creel is more than likely an old Penobscot Indian relic. She said her husband has a new one he bought last year at the Indian Island Reservation Store, and it has the same weave pattern. She was pretty certain it was Penobscot. But that's not what got us curious. Look inside, please."

A dozen or so very small, rocky nuggets fell out into DeLyon's hand. He recognized them immediately. "Do you have any idea where this creel was found?"

"I found it," Charlie said, somewhat excitedly. "It was under some old boards in the shed, hidden inside an old bag."

Marie added, "We think it was simply left there unintentionally—perhaps one of those out-of-sight-out-of-mind things. But by who, and when, is uncertain. That river feeds into the Penobscot, and we always understood that the whole area was once tribal territory."

"From what you are telling me, it is entirely possible that this creel and the stones it contains came from the esker right on your property, or perhaps very close to it. We here in the Geology Department have been studying that gravel ridge line—which, by the way is more than 140 miles long from north to south, for many years. We often turn up evidence of habitation by the Penobscots ... things such as arrowheads, stone tools, and other man-made items.

I won't bore you with technical details, but those gravel ridges—and Maine has dozens and dozens of them, especially in the eastern and southeastern areas, are the remaining evidence of the glacial ice shield that once covered this State."

"I learned something about that, through Charlie," Marie said. "He and his classmates had a school project last year, where they took a map of North America and colored it to show how far the ice advanced south. He said to me, 'Mom, you won't believe this! Where you grew up had ice on it two miles high!' He was pointing at northern New England on his map. Of course it also covered most of Wisconsin, too."

———

"That's right, Charlie," DeLyon said. "That all happened, and ended, more than 12,000 years ago."

Turning to Marie, he said, "But you didn't come here today to talk about the ice age, I presume. You want to know about these stones."

"Yes, we do. The manager at the hotel where we are staying back in Moreville suggested this visit. We didn't show him the stones, but we asked who would know the most about rocks in the State of Maine. He said you folks would be the ones to talk to."

"Well, he's right. We are. And, if you'll come back up to the lab with me, I'll help you find out exactly what these stones are."

Back in the lab on the second floor, with Marie and Charlie watching, DeLyon carefully placed the stones—twelve in total, on a round, metal plate. They were very small, not quite clear, and might be mistaken for glass—without the telltale greenish tint on the inside. Picking up one of the stones, he said, "I'll be using a checklist of some simple steps I'll take to show us what kind of stone we have here," although he was all but certain he already knew what he had in his hand.

"First thing we do is weigh it," he said, gently placing the object on a nearby scale and getting a reading of .06 grams.

"Now we will get a measurement." Using a set of complicated looking calipers, the stone measured about 3.8 millimeters. "Next we will see how hard it is. I have a small strip of corundum, which is a very hard material, attached to this board. If we can scratch it with this rock, then we know its hardness exceeds corundum." Holding it in a special gripping tool, DeLyon firmly dragged a pointed corner of the stone across the strip of corundum. First he touched the corundum with his finger to see if he could feel the scratch mark.

"There is a mark," he announced. "See if you can feel it," he said, indigent both Marie and Charlie to touch the surface with their fingers.

"Yes, I can feel it," Charlie replied. "Yes, I can also feel it," Marie added.

"Next is specific gravity," DeLyon said "but that takes a bit of time and so we'll reserve that for later—if it becomes necessary at all. So, now we'll check it for thermal absorption, or heat transfer.

I have this device here, which looks like of like a soldering gun. If I hold it to the stone and press this button ... it shows me a reading of ... 22 watts per centimeter Kelvin.

And, finally, the check for light refraction." DeLyon, using special tweezers, held the stone close to the lens of an instrument that looked like a small flashlight emitting a thin beam of light toward the ceiling. Looking down onto the stone, and gently rocking it in the beam, he said, "and there's my rainbow."

He invited Marie and Charlie to observe for themselves what he was seeing. "I can see it," Marie said. "Red, blue, green, and maybe even yellow. Oh, and a bit of purple."

Charlie took a quick look and said, "Mom! That's just what I saw the other day when you held one of the stones up to the sun!

"And, now, if you haven't already guessed, what kind of stones do you think these are?" DeLyon asked.

"Diamonds?" Marie tentatively offered.

"Yes," DeLyon replied. "I can say with certainty that you have as small collection here of what are called alluvial diamonds. That is because of where they more than likely were found—somewhere along that gravel ridge by the River. The tests I just ran were all tests for diamonds, which is what I recognized them to be when I first saw your 'stones.' They are harder than corundum, which is a 9 on the hardness scale, with diamonds being 10. They tested correctly on the thermal absorption scale, and they refract light into rainbow colors—as they should.

As to value, that is not something we do here. You'd have to take them to a jeweler for that—if you're interested, of course."

"How about the creel? Can you tell us how old it is?" Marie asked.

"We would have to carbon date it. That's done in another lab, and I'd have to see if we could fit that in our schedule. Perhaps you would leave it with me, now, and I'll call you later with the results of the testing. In fact, if I might, I would also you to consider donating the creel to our Department. We can call it an artifact under study by our glacial geology students. I can contact you how?" DeLyon inquired.

Marie wrote down her Aunt Ellie's phone number in Wisconsin on a notepad.

"And, yes, please keep the creel. I'm sure there are people who will find it of interest—perhaps the Penobscot people on the Island. By the way, have you and your colleagues found diamonds like these here in Maine?"

"Yes, we have, although alluvial diamonds are rare and very hard to find. A couple of big ones were located here in the U.S. back in the 1800's: one in Wisconsin; and two or three others in Indiana. Interestingly, neither state has kimberlites, where most diamonds originate on the earth's surface. Just like yours, they came from someplace in Canada. There are a number of projects underway up there to locate kimberlites.

In simple terms, there are two families of diamonds: those mined in the ground directly from kimberlite rock; and those on the surface, separated from their kimberlite origin by some means and transported by ice and water to some, new location—often some distance away.

In fact, on a recent pipeline survey project I worked on in northern Quebec, one of our team happened to see some alluvial diamonds while visiting a friend at McGill University. They were found in south-central Quebec in roadside till—that's residue left from the movement by the ice shield. I didn't actually see them, but my boss on that project, Mel Johnson, told me about it. He's from Maine, too, by the way. He works out of an office down in Massachusetts, but he also has offices in Portland and up in Quebec City." He gave Marie the address of the company's web site.

"And this fellow Johnson: how old might he be?" Marie inquired as casually as possible.

"Not sure, but I'd say early 30's. Why do you ask?"

"Oh, nothing. I may have known someone by that name, that's all." *Oh my lord, is it possible it's him?"*

Marie's Challenge

University of Chicago Law School

The Grants Office manager at the Law School told Marie she only had to give them an overview of her proposed project, and they would help her do the rest: identify one or more likely sponsors, and guide her through the application process.

Marie did her best thinking when she was busy, and now, behind the wheel of big John Deere tractor, pulling a 5-bottom switch plow through the rich, dark Wisconsin soil on her aunt Ellie's farm, she was doing her best to concentrate on keeping her rows straight— trying not to think of her challenge.

It was mid-morning of an early fall day, and after reaching the row's end in front of the stream which defined the farm's property line and making a full turn, she paused, pushed the lever to reverse the plow's blades, left them in the raised position, pulled the throttle to idle, and then shut off the engine.

She poured herself a cup of hot coffee from a thermos and climbed down to the ground. Walking to the front of the tractor, she leaned against the block of counterweights and looked back to the west, where she could just make out the roof of the barn.

Ok, we found some stones in Maine that turned out to be diamonds. And in the process learned that they were transported there, by the glacial ice shield, eons earlier. From Quebec.

And these things ended up on the lands of Native Americans.

Indians. Like me, and like my son Charlie. At least, in part ... but ... that isn't really relevant. What is important is where the stones came from. Quebec. A huge Province. One of Canada's largest. And where they came from is the traditional homeland of the Inuit and the Cree. Aboriginals, in many ways not unlike the Penobscots. And traditional homelands which were, for centuries, wild, undeveloped, unspoiled, and rich in resources from which they supported their subsistence lifestyle.

Would it have mattered if either or both peoples knew such stones were valuable before the white man came? No, of course not. From everything I've read so far, what mattered to them were birch trees for building canoes; caribou and deer meat for sustenance and their bones and horns for tool making; whales and seals for lamp oil and food for their families and their sled dogs; and fish and clams and rabbits and birds and walrus to fill out their diet. And beyond their use as simple tools and hunting weapons, and a small number for art objects, they didn't care much about earthly stones.

What also mattered was their freedom to live as nomads, moving with the seasons and organizing their lives around the migration of birds and land animals and lake and river and sea creatures. They had no sense of ownership, and they were unschooled, but they were superior custodians of their lands and all it contained. They knew how to sustain themselves and at the same time protect what was important and useful.

Okay, so, now we come to the present. The Inuit, the Cree, and the Penobscot ... and other tribes for that matter, have been forced to sign treaties with their respective Governments and give up all 'ownership' to their homelands—which of course they never actually 'owned' in the first place. And, in the process, they gave up any right they might have had to the land-born natural resources ... except, of course, on their self-governed reservations.

Does anybody care about this? What do we know now that they didn't know at the time?

Marie finished her coffee, restarted the tractor, dropped the plow blades and began the return run. She was halfway to the end when she had another insight, suddenly remembering something Dr. DeLyon had said.

He said there's a difference between diamonds found in the ground ... from kimberlites, he said ... and alluvial diamonds, like the one's Charlie found ... that were carried away from the kimberlite sites by ice and water. One, you dig for, and the other you simply pick out of gravel already on the ground ... that is, if you can find them at all.

The question is: is it possible to make a case out of that difference?

At the end of the field nearest the barn, she spotted her aunt Ellie, signaling with her straw hat. Minutes later, as Marie dropped to the ground in front of the barn, aunt Ellie told her about the phone call.

The report from DeWalt Realty was certainly good news: her inherited property had sold, netting her just over $150,000. This meant she could pay off her school loan, with a good amount left over.

More good news came days later when a letter from the Law School Grant's Office in Chicago, invited her to a meeting two days hence with a potential sponsor of her grant application, The Robert Wood Johnson Foundation. She realized, however, that the original motivation for seeking to join a non-profit organization as a means of forgiving her debt was now moot. Nonetheless, having devoted so much time and effort to the project, she decided to continue what she had started.

On the appointed day, she left Charlie in her aunt Ellie's care and made the trip to Chicago, not altogether certain that she was prepared for the meeting. At the Grant's Office, she was greeted and shown to a small conference room, where she was introduced to a Mr. Mikael Tremblay. Tremblay, who was a foot shorter than Marie, was smartly dressed in a Navy blazer displaying a Foundation patch, white dress shirt with a striped tie, well-shined dress shoes, and light brown slacks. His name appeared on a metal, gold-colored nametag attached above the blazer's pocket.

"Good morning, Ms. Webber. My name is Mikael Tremblay and I'm here representing The Robert Wood Johnson Foundation. And, please, call me Mikael." Hmmm, he sounds French, Marie thought.

After an exchange of handshakes, Marie replied, "Good morning to you, Mikael, and thank you for your interest. This is my first foray into the world of grants, and I only hope I was able to present a convincing case. And, please, it's Marie."

"Let me begin by telling you that we were quite impressed with your proposal, Marie. What I'd like to know is how you came up with the idea? I don't think we've ever seen anything quite like it."

"What I did was put together the history of development in the northeast of the US and its impact on aboriginal culture and life in parallel with similar development efforts and impact in the Nunavik now underway in contemporary times.

First, as I noted in my proposal, following the end of the last ice age and before the presence of Europeans or anyone from outside North America, the northeastern area of the US, the Maritime Provinces, and part of Quebec Province south of the St. Lawrence, was the home of the Wabanaki Nation Indians.

———————

Beginning in the 17th Century, Europeans began the occupation of these traditional homelands and discovering for themselves a wealth of resources, from timber to fish to land animals. In addition to the exploitation of those resources, of course, the diseases they introduced decimated the Native American population. And it was immediately evident that Indians were simply unprepared to compete or assimilate with their more modernized occupiers.

Eventually, as we all know, a series of treaties were executed over time and in stages that resulted in the reduction of those original, native homelands to small, isolated reservations. The vast majority of those lands are now contained under State, Provincial, or private control.

I was struck by the similarity between this history and what is now occurring in northern Quebec. As I summarized in my proposal, this has been going on for a long time, beginning with whaling and fur trading, hydroelectric production, and more recently the exploitation of non-renewable resources through mining and other extraction activity.

The result of all this is alarmingly similar to what previously occurred on Native American homelands. While it is understandable that the Canadian and Provincial governments wish to see their lands developed, the end result is that the Cree and Inuit population has been forced to abandon their nomadic ways and adjust to life in small, reservation-style villages. And, as with the case of Native Americans, the lack of formal education and modern skills have left them woefully unprepared to compete.

In the drive to become energy independent—and, of course, generate royalties, and licensing and tax revenues from private investors and operators, it is not surprising that governments in the U.S. and Canada are actively supporting what is being called economic development efforts. In more practical terms, this means that every effort is being made to locate and recover non-renewable resources—often, in my opinion, in ways that minimize the objections of the public and in particular those on whose traditional lands those very resources are being discovered and harvested.

Behind my proposal are the two propositions that underlie all such efforts: one, that when people in the modern era profitably exploit the non-renewable resources from the traditional homelands of aboriginal peoples, there should be a legal, guaranteed, and fair share of any profits awarded to those aboriginals—all those aboriginals; and, two, that every effort should be made to preserve and protect the land and waters as well as the bird, fish and wildlife and other renewable resources that have for centuries supported a traditional culture and way of life."

"Yes, I understand that much. It's the next part that got our attention. How did you come up with that?" Mikael asked.

"You remember I mentioned that my son and I found some stones, which turned out to be diamonds, on our property in Maine? Well, although both he and I share a Native American heritage: I'm part Maliseet, and he's part Penobscot; I decided to see if they could be shared. But shared with whom? Sure, they ended up in Maine, but all the evidence suggests they came from Quebec."

"Interesting you should mention your heritage," Tremblay said. "My mother is a Cree, and my father is a French Canadian as it gets, so I am technically a Metis, or 'of mixed blood.' I was born in western Quebec, near James Bay, in the village of Chisasib. My wife and I now live in Quebec City. I am quite familiar with much of the land you are talking about in your proposal."

Marie continued, "To understand all this, I quickly learned that I need to find out a lot more about land claim agreements and treaties at both ends of the journey my stones took. In the transition from traditional homelands to State or Provincial land, of course, the aboriginals gave up their rights to all resources present on those lands.

But I'm uncertain as to whether or not those agreements and treaties account for treasures that have been moved around. Or, as a Glacial Geologists at the University of Maine put it: most valuable minerals, in particular diamonds, are recovered at the point of their origin, in the earth's surface from what are known as kimberlites. Others, however rare, are merely picked up off the ground, having been transported far away from the point of origin by ice and water. They are referred to as alluvial, and precisely where they came from is not an easy thing to establish."

"Except, as you said, in your case, you know the ones you found came from Quebec." Tremblay said.

"Yes, indeed. And I was able to put together this crude map of where, in Quebec, they most like originated. The red line indicates the general direction of the ice shield as it passed back and forth over Quebec and northern New England."

———

"So, somewhere on that line, your diamonds emerged from the mantle to the surface in a kimberlite, where they and a lot of other junk were picked up over time by glaciers, transported south, and deposited in your back yard when the ice melted. That about it?" Tremblay asked.

"Yep. You get the picture. Remember, though, there are no known kimberlite sites in Maine, but there are several in Quebec. Any alluvial diamonds found in Maine, therefore, had to come from Quebec. And, I know a Glacial Geologist who says he can prove it."

"And that's why, in your proposal, you used the phrase "Sharing Ice Age Resources in the 21st Century."

"Correct. And to be clear, the case I'm hoping to build on is that these alluvial treasures ... well, perhaps that's being overly generous ... after I had my diamonds assayed they turned out to be worth only a few hundred dollars. Anyway, it would be next to impossible to directly link them to any one of the known, kimberlite sites. It could be any one of them, one not yet discovered, or perhaps even more than one."

"Ah, I think I'm beginning to see where you're going with this," Tremblay said. "Those diamonds now being mined from the ground in Quebec are covered by mining claims agreements. But others, like the ones you found, may not be."

"That's correct, and because they're byproducts of the ice age, I'm calling them 'Ice Age Resources.' And, I feel strongly that they should be shared—land claims agreements or mining claims notwithstanding. The challenge now is to see if I can develop a legally grounded case, identify and enlighten the proper spokespersons, and then convince them to take the case to the legislative bodies who make the laws and formulate mining regulations."

"You suggest you can do this in two years?"

"Yes, with some help, of course."

"A worthy objective, and one that I strongly feel the Foundation will be willing to support. It was a pleasure meeting you, Marie, and I thank you for your time today. You will be hearing from us shortly after our Board meeting early next month," Tremblay replied.

As she left the building, Marie thought to herself, *I just might be in over my head on this one.*

Canadian Law

Ottawa, Canada

Marie knew enough about U.S. property law from her legal studies to know that anyone who files a property claim is saying 'I want control over this land, including any bodies of water on or adjoining it.' She also knew that if the land happens to have never been subject to governmental sovereignty, it was often considered to be *terrae nullius*, or 'nobody's land,' and acquired merely by the act of occupancy, which made control a simple matter.

For centuries upon centuries following the retreat of the last ice shield some 12,000 years ago, the land we now know as North America was certainly occupied, as the earliest settlers from Europe and elsewhere immediately discovered. To the aboriginals who lived there, the notion of land ownership was as alien as the white faces they later confronted.

Marie knew she had a lot more to learn about land and mining claims, particular in Canada. This led to an invitation to visit Ottawa, at the invitation of a Professor from Ottawa University's Law Center on 57 Louis Pasteur Street, well known for its strong focus on public-interest law.

Although he wasn't at all pleased about it, Charlie would have to remain behind on the farm with his great-aunt Ellie as his mother set off on her quest. She wasn't at all sure just how long she might be away. It was early fall, a Saturday, and forecasts called for seasonal temperatures and good weather, so Marie chose to drive rather than fly. She stopped for the night in London, Ontario, and reached the Canadian Capitol by mid-afternoon on Sunday.

At the recommendation of her contact at the University of Ottawa's Law Center, she located and checked into the King Edward B&B on King Edward Avenue near the Law School. She settled in, went to a nearby café where she enjoyed a light evening meal, and back at B&B spent some time reviewing her notes for the next day's appointment with Dr. Michelle Parsons, Professor of Public Interest Law.

In the morning, wearing her usual long sleeved blouse under a light sweater, denim slacks and leather jacket, she made the short walk to the Law School, arriving for her 8:30 appointment on time. She was directed to a suite of offices on the second floor. Midway down a wide hallway, she found her host's door open. Stepping in, she saw that the Professor was on the phone, her free hand motioning for Marie to enter and then pointing to a seating area near the doorway.

Before Marie had finished taking off her jacket, Dr. Parsons ended her call, picked up a document from her desk, and came to greet her. "Sorry about the interruption. That was Sam, my 10 year old, all in a dither. Couldn't find the socks he always wears to after-school hockey practice," Parsons said. "Apparently it didn't occur to him to check the laundry room," she ended with a grin. "Oh, the trials and tribulations of a single mother."

"No problem," Marie replied with a wide smile. "I know all about 10 year olds and their collections of favorite things. I have one of my own. His name is Charlie. A friend once told me that when it comes to raising children the first twenty five year are the most fun."

"Oh, Lord. That's too much to think about," Parsons answered with a chuckle. "Anyway, welcome to Ottawa. It's a lovely Monday morning, and sadly, I have to start off with some bad news: I had hoped to be free for the next couple of days, but the replacement I had arrange to take over my classes for today and Wednesday came down with the flu. So, I have only an hour before my first class.

Now I know you are a recent graduate from one of the finest Schools of Law in the States, and well-schooled in U.S. law. The letter of introduction and the copy of your grant you sent me suggest you've already done some initial research and prepared yourself as best as you can.

But, as one lawyer to another, and certainly no disrespect intended, you wouldn't be here today if you were satisfied that that preparation was fully adequate. So, to get you up to speed and for me to be able to be most helpful, I've arranged a 72-hour crash course in Canadian history and law and organized a collection of relevant materials and documents for you to look over.

You're invited to make yourself comfortable in our very fine Law Library, and the Reference Clerk happens to be my sister-in-law. She's already arranged a good deal of information for you, so you won't need to spend any time searching. And she'll be a great help finding anything else you may wish to examine. Hopefully, your schedule will allow for this change?"

"Thank you. I have a more or less open schedule, and I will use the time well. And, yes, there's only so much I was able to do from a distance."

"Speaking of which, you traveled some distance already just getting here. Why don't we finish our chat this morning over a cup of coffee at the Café on the ground level? I usually visit there before my class, and it's right next to the Library."

"That sounds good. By the way, that B&B you recommended served us a wonderful breakfast this morning, but their coffee wasn't so great. I could use a decent cup."

As they approached the Café, Professor Parsons said, "I understand you plan to do some traveling in northern Quebec."

"Yes, I do, eventually."

"Now that will give you a whole new appreciation for travel distances. That Province is immense, and you'd better go prepared for some serious winter weather. And that's not an overstatement."

———————

For the next three days and a good portion of two evenings, Marie immersed herself in things Canadian. For the rest of Monday, she went through documents on the history of Quebec, from the arrival of the French in the 16th Century, to the takeover by the British, and the eventual establishment of Canada as a Dominion of the Commonwealth. She reviewed documents on the evolution of Provincial development in the region known as 'lower Canada' and, for Quebec, the expansion of its land area during the 20th Century, until it became the largest of Canada's 14 Provinces.

She also reviewed the history of federal voting rights for Canadian minorities including peoples of the First Nations, the Inuit, and the Metis, and the ongoing conflicts with these populations over their rights to self-governance—specifically in the north, or 'upper Canada.'

She was struck, once again, by the realities of aboriginal transition from a nomadic lifestyle, where they made a living from renewable and carefully protected natural resources, to one of dependency and subsistence living in isolated reserves, and the similarities with experiences of Native Americans in the U.S. There were, however, some important and critical differences she planned to examine further.

Most of the second day was spent reviewing the history of the James Bay and subsequent Comprehensive Land Claims Agreements, some of the regulations on different types of mining claims, and other more specific land claims resulting in the establishment of parks, wildlife sanctuaries, and other public facilities.

The last and third day was focused on documents relating to aboriginal self-governance as well as groups and organizations established to represent their interests. The more she read, the more confused she got. It was a complex and ever-changing subject, and it was difficult to track. The myriad of so-called representative groups had stated purposes ranging from economic development, to women's concerns, to housing and health care, to education and training, to the preservation of native languages and customs, and to public safety and policing. Some were governmental organizations at the Crown level, others at the Provincial level, and others at the municipal level. Some groups were non-profit NGOs, others might be called 'interest groups,' while others were public corporations.

By the time Marie finished, on Wednesday evening, however, she felt she was much better prepared to proceed. But she also humbled by knowing there was so very much more to learn. All in all, she was pleased to be on her way.

Before finding a place to have dinner and settling in for the night, she called home, bringing her aunt Ellie up to date and spending some time chatting with her son, Charlie. He seemed to be doing ok with her absence, happily occupied with school and chores on the farm, but what had really captured his attention was a new orphaned yellow lab puppy that aunt Ellie had taken in.

"I named him Fred," Charlie reported. "You know why, Mom?"

"'Cause he looks just like your old teddy bear?" she replied, all but certain she was correct.

"Yeah. How did you guess?"

"Oh, there are just some things that only Moms know," she replied, smiling. "I'll call you again in a few days, Charlie. Goodnight sweetheart. I love you."

———

When Marie reached Dr. Parson's office on Thursday morning, she was somewhat surprised to find two other people in the office. "Good morning, Ms. Webber," Parsons said. "You look ready to continue. I trust you used the past three days to your advantage."

"Yes, I did, and my thanks to your sister-in-law. She was a great help." *I wonder who these people are,* Marie is thinking as she looked at the two strangers.

"Good. Well, before we get started," Parsons said, pointing to the two guests, "I want to introduce you to two of our visiting post-doc Fellows. They come to us from McGill University."

Indicating the first of the two guests, she said, "Say hello to Louise Pelletier, from Mt. Laurier, Quebec, and this," indicating the second guest, "is Pierre Corriveau, from Quebec City. Louise is a specialist in Constitutional Law, and Pierre specializes in Aboriginal Law."

Marie shook hands with both, saying, "Good morning, Louise … and Pierre." *Aaaahh, they're from Quebec. I understand now.*

Parsons continued, "I took the liberty of sharing your project with them. Both said they are willing to assist, as time permits, of course. Their legal expertise, which is substantial, should give you considerable help, but perhaps equally important, as natives of Quebec, they have first-hand knowledge of and experience in the very landscape you are hoping to understand."

Somewhat humbled, Marie said, "I suppose I should first thank you in advance for your help. As you may know, I haven't yet had the pleasure of visiting Quebec, although I grew up in Maine and was surrounded by it on three sides. After what I've been doing for the past three days, I recognize just how much I still have to learn. Perhaps we can find some time to get together one evening while I'm here? I was thinking of leaving . . ."

Before Louise or Pierre could respond, Parsons interjected, "As a matter of fact, let's do this: let's all meet at my home tomorrow evening. You three can get to know each other a little better, and perhaps share contact information. My son and I would love the company. We're having spaghetti and meatballs, his favorite, of course."

All three replied, almost in unison, "Good idea!"

————

After Pierre and Louise excused themselves, Parsons asked Marie what she thought about her 'crash course.' "That was hard work," Marie replied. "I felt like was back in Law School."

"That was the intention," Parsons answered. "Now, you said you came to us to learn more about Canadian Land Claim Agreements, and how they may differ from those in the States."

"Yes, that's where I'm beginning," Marie replied. "One of the main things I learned over the past three days is that my limited exposure to constitutional law and property law only scratched the surface of what I need to know. And, you mentioned that Pierre is an expert in aboriginal law and policies. I have a lot of catching up to do on that topic.

I also was struck by how land claim Agreements here in Canada have served to fundamentally change the way the Country and its Provinces and Territories relate to its minority populations and their traditional homelands."

"They certainly did, but it's important to see it in the context of Quebec's history in dealing with its aboriginals." And for the rest of the morning, Dr. Parsons and Marie reviewed the Province's history, beginning with the arrival of the French in the 17th Century, the later takeover by the British.

Dr. Parsons handed Marie a document, explaining that it was a copy of a recent address given by an Associate Chief Judge on the topic.

"I think you'll find this of interest, especially because the Judge, himself, is an Aboriginal from the Ojibway Tribe in Manitoba. You can read it later."

"It must have been interesting when it occurred to elected representatives and officials in high office that the expanded Province now included two new groups of aboriginal citizens who already had their own government," Marie said.

"Well, perhaps, but again, you have to understand the context in which all this was taking place. You see, 95% of Quebec's population lives in the southern region along the St Lawrence on less than 10% of all available land. Outside this area, you have a combination of vast uninhabited areas, a scattering of smaller villages and towns, large boreal forests, treeless taiga, and finally, lots and lots of arctic tundra."

"And most folks in the south were and, perhaps still are, unfamiliar with their own country to the north, and rarely if ever traveled there, I take it," Marie replied.

"Quite true, and what we now call 'upper Canada,' especially the Yukon and the Northwest Territories, is even less well known. And, of course, as you now know, the first to show interest in the north did so because of what they began to discover it had to offer, beginning with whaling and fur trading. Later, it was hydroelectric power, timber, ground based minerals, and an assortment of other commercially attractive resources. For instance, you will notice that among the parties who signed the James Bay Agreement were three public energy corporations."

"I did note that," Marie replied.

They paused for a short lunch break in the School's Cafeteria, and continued their conversation back in Parsons' office.

"I presume you now understand the distinction between 'Comprehensive Land Claims,' and those of a more specific nature, such as mining claims, claims to establish public parks, and so on. Some specific claims are made based on failure of the Provincial government to fulfill its obligations under prior treaties or comprehensive agreements. In both types of claims, however, the rights and interests of aboriginals who may be affected are spelled out in detail.

I have a map here I'll show you where Canada has worked out Comprehensive Land Claim Agreements with aboriginal communities.

––––––––––

As to more recent mining claims in Quebec, I understand there are a large number of active mines in Quebec, but currently only one for diamonds. There is a lot of mineral prospecting going on up there, and if one believes the publicity on the subject, there may well be more diamonds discovered in the future."

"It looks like that map pretty much covers all of what you said before was referred to as 'Upper Canada.' Now, am I correct in understanding that a specific land claim, such as those you mentioned, are arranged within the context of the previous Comprehensive Agreements?" Marie asked.

"Yes, and that attaches a constitutional element that wouldn't be there otherwise. We'll go over that more with Louise when we get together."

"Ok, now, as to a specific mining claim, how does that work, exactly?"

"There are two types of claims: Lode Claims and Placer Claims. Lode implies a vein or lode, with a well-defined boundary, typically sized in the order of 300 by 1,500 feet. Placer implies unconsolidated, or distributed deposits, and claims can be from 20 to 160 acres in size.

Usually, activity begins with an interested party obtaining a prospector's license, whether it be one or more individuals or a corporation. If sampling and testing identifies a proven deposit, then it largely becomes a matter of economics: what level of investment will it take to recover the deposit, and so on. And, of course, there are other issues to consider such as free access and transportation, infrastructure, environmental protection, royalties, permits, and so on. Mining regulations here in Canada is a lively subject, not easily understood, and continuing to evolve.

Mining is done on what is called a 'staked' claim, ranging in size from 40 to more than 1,200 acres. The claim holder is required to install actual, physical markers on the ground to identify the claim's boundaries, but these days most corporations use what is called 'map staking,' or laying out the land area of interest on a survey map. They don't even have to have visited the site.

Since more than 90% of the land in northern Quebec is owned by the Province, the mining companies are permitted to 'lease' the land for their operations, usually for a 20 year period and renewable in 10 year increments."

After absorbing this, Marie said, "That is helpful, and leads me to the central issue in my project. To explain, let me share with you a story about how I became interested in land claims." And for the next several minutes, she went on to recount how, during the sale of inherited property in Maine, her son had come upon some diamond nuggets. She recounted her interest in sharing what she called 'ice age treasures.'"

"That's quite a story, I must say," Parsons said, after Marie had finished. "And, now, you are hoping to take this further and do what, exactly?"

"Honestly, I'm not yet sure, and that's why I came here. As I said in my Grant proposal, I'm trying to see if there is a way to ensure that such treasures are recognized as dynamic and unique ice-age products, no longer attached to any given host source that is now or might someday be part of a specific land or mining claim. And, moreover, that no matter where they may be discovered—on Provincial, State, community, or privately owned lands, it is important to recognize that their journey began and ended on the traditional, aboriginal homeland of the Cree, the Inuit, and the Wabanakis."

"You know," Parsons said, as the afternoon session was winding down, "I have an idea, and it has to do with Placer Claims. I'll have to do some more research, but why don't we do this: let's get Pierre and Louise in on the discussion tomorrow evening over dinner."

Back in Marblehead

Marblehead, Massachusetts

Mel awoke early, as usual, and made the short walk from his condo to his office at the waterfront, overlooking the harbor. On the way, he stopped in at the Harbor's Edge Restaurant for his favorite breakfast of hot oatmeal, a side of crispy bacon, and homemade cinnamon-raisin toast.

When he entered his office, he noted that Martha had prepped the coffee maker, so he pushed the start button and waited a few minutes to enjoy a cup of his favorite Dunkin Donut brand. He was feeling good, knowing his team would be arriving in a week to review progress on the Quebec project. Mel planned to spend the morning contacting each of them for an update and assigning a topic for their presentation at the upcoming meeting.

Just then he noticed a package that Martha had apparently put on his desk sometime late yesterday, probably after he had left early to have his car serviced. It was from Mark DeLyon, and contained a well-organized and thorough report on the geological aspects of each of the three sites visited on their recent trip to the Nunavik. It also included a map, illustrating the prospective pipeline routes that Roy Martin had given them, highlighting all known glacial features, in detail, along the way, including eskers and moraines, drumlins, cirques, horns, arêtes, and talus deposits.

He reached John Jenkins mid-morning at their branch office in

Portland, Maine. "Hey, John. I'm putting together the agenda for our get-together next week next on the Quebec job, so tell me what you're preparing to talk about."

"Hey, Mel. Well, I just got in the day before yesterday from a week in San Antonio. As you always say: don't reinvent wheels. So, I was able to catch up with an old friend who is with Valero. Got to spend some time with their planners along with some visiting pipe experts from the Enbridge Corporation. They were more than willing to share what they have learned about requirements for pipe engineering and arctic infrastructure, so we now have a leg up. I was also able to get up to speed on the specs for Enbridge's Line 9 extension to Montreal, where the product will be transported by ship to the refineries at Levis on Quebec City's south shore. I'll be covering that in detail."

"What about TransCanada's plans? Anything new there?"

"According to Valero's people, TransCanada has a plan in the works they're calling 'Energy East,' with a proposed new line to bring both gas and oil from western Canada, but Valero isn't buying in. They already plan to ship product between Montreal and Quebec City, and the oil they're talking about is that tar sands stuff. It's not without its own controversies. And, as you know, TransCanada's Keystone Project is on hold. I'll make sure to cover that at our meeting."

"Ok, good, John. Look forward to seeing you soon."

A few minutes later he reached Billy Poulin, who was in his car on the way back from a week in Quebec City. "Good morning, Billy. I see I've caught you on the move. I'm putting the agenda together for our meeting next week and need to know what you'll be covering."

"Yeah, Mel. 'Morning to you, too. Well, from everything I've learned, it appears the existing storage facilities in Quebec City will soon be at maximum capacity, what with Valero planning on transshipping from Montreal, and some continued inflow from abroad. So, what I've been looking at are sites for new tanks and available docks for off-loading. Looks like we'll need to plan for new structures and hookups.

I'll be bringing the details and can speak to what I've been able to find, so far at least."

"Ok, good, Billy. See you in a week. You on your way home now?"

"Yes, but I'm planning to stop in Portland on the way. I'll be taking a look at what's going on there, since Phil mentioned his desire for a future line direct from Quebec. Such a line, by the way, will most likely have a direct impact on what we suggest needs to be done in Quebec City, so it's a matter of timing, as I see it."

"I agree. It's a balancing act, for sure," Mel replied. "Drive safely, and say hello to your good wife for me."

"Will do."

Unable to reach the third member of his team, Eddy Burns, Mel left a voice-mail message and a request for a return call as soon as he was able to go over the agenda. As he was finishing the call, Martha arrived.

"Good morning and welcome back, boss," she said, her arms full of mail along with a large flower arrangement. "I thought these might brighten up the place a bit. With the fall days getting shorter all the time, it can be sort of gloomy down here in the harbor. And, besides, where you've just come from, I don't suppose there were many of these about."

"You're right there, MOM," Mel answered. "When you get above the tree line, it seems pretty gloomy all the time."

"Well, I had better get to work on your travel expenses. You did keep all your receipts, didn't you?"

"Yes, I did, but give me a few minutes to get them organized. And, while we're on the subject of travel, I'll be giving you some information for planning my next trip. This time I'll be going even further north—in about three weeks, to a new territorial area called the Nunavut. Please reach out to Mark DeLyon and see if he's free to join me. He said he thought he might be before we left each other in Montreal, but needed to check on some things at the University before he could commit to the schedule.

I was impressed with him, by the way. I'll talk to the others before hand, but I'm thinking of making him an offer to join us. We could use a full time Geologist on the team. And, speaking about

Geology, remind me to tell you later on about catching up with Roger Gagnon, one of my former students who's now at McGill."

Dinner Date

Ottawa, Ontario

On Friday evening, following a hand-drawn map and detailed directions, Marie left the King Edward B&B and traveled a few miles west along Wellington Street and then onto the Sir John A. McDonald Parkway, arriving in front of Dr. Parson's home at the corner of Lyndale and Stonehurst Avenues, overlooking Larouche Park.

She recognized that she was the last to arrive, noting the two other cars with Quebec plates already parked at the curb at the end of the driveway. The home was on the small side, fronted by a neat yard containing a pair of large maple trees, and seemed well suited to its historic Ashburham neighborhood.

Young Sam greeted Marie at the door and welcomed her to his and his mother's home. After a brief handshake, she handed him a gift bottle of wine as he led her to the kitchen. There, with wine glasses in hand, Pierre and Louise were watching their host prepare a mixed green salad.

"Marie's here," Sam announced.

"Sam!" his mother said. "She's Ms. Webber to you. My goodness. Where are your manners?"

"But she said I was to call her Marie," Sam answered, somewhat taken aback and looking to Marie for confirmation.

Marie smiled and nodded. "Yes, I did. Sorry, 'Mom.'"

Michelle also smiled and nodded, indicating all was well. And she saw that her son Sam had relaxed, quickly returning to his usual, easygoing manner.

Following a lovely meal of spaghetti and meatballs, salad, garlic bread, and a slice of homemade apple pie with ice cream, Sam was excused to watch his favorite TV show before bedtime. The four adults served themselves a fresh cup of coffee and moved to the living room at the front of the house overlooking the Park.

Dr. Parsons spent a few minutes bringing Pierre and Louise up to date on the discussions she and Marie had been having, and soon after there was a lively four-way exchange of information and ideas. *This is like being in a seminar, Marie thought, except this one includes two single moms.*

Pierre asked Marie to provide some more detail about the discovery of diamond nuggets on her property in Maine. After she did so, he said, "So, all the evidence suggests that your treasures came out of a ridge of gravel, apparently first found by some unknown Penobscot and then later re-discovered by someone in your family. They were found on as opposed to in the ground. Am I not correct?"

"Yes, according to what a Geologist told me," Marie replied. "They are clearly glacial alluvials, and from what I remember about what he said, they were brought to the earth's surface millions of years ago in a kimberlite host rock, then separated from that host over time, picked up along with other loose material known as till, transported by ice and water, and ultimately re-deposited elsewhere—in fact, as it so happened, into what was once my own back yard."

Louise then spoke up and said, "Beyond the matter of location, I suggest we might examine this in the context of time as well. What I mean is: your nuggets surfaced in Quebec millions of years ago, as you explained, and then perhaps millions of years afterward, ended up in Maine. Call that the geological history.

Later, the lands where they began that journey became the traditional homelands of the Inuit and Cree, and the lands where they ended up were home to ... what did you call them, the Wabanakis ... the Penobscot Tribe are part of that Confederation, I presume ... anyway, home to Native Americans. This history goes back ... what ... twelve thousand years or more? Call that the aboriginal history.

So, now, seen in the present context, your treasures started out on land controlled one way or the other by the Federal and Provincial government, and ended up on land controlled in one way or the other by the State. In northern Quebec, the process of gaining control through Comprehensive Land Claim Agreements included adoption of the terms by legislative action, giving them the force of law. I suggest something similar happened in Maine through the treatise process.

Therefore, it may be necessary to examine more carefully how those Agreements and Treatises on both sides of the border are amended, or altered."

————

Dr. Parsons said, "Marie and I earlier were talking about mining claims, and I had only a brief look into the subject, but I did learn that the majority of diamond mining claims in Quebec are for what are called lode deposits, and what we're talking about here would be considered placer deposits. We'll need to look into the Mining Act and mine regulations to understand better how claims work there, but what are we talking about here where it concerns Marie's project? A change of some kind to the Mining Act, or a rider of some type to the regulations, or perhaps even some kind of bi-lateral resolution between the Canadian and US governments?"

Louise responded, "At the moment I don't think we know enough to say whether or not any one of those ideas is the best, or even an appropriate, course to consider. I mean, can we say with certainty that Marie's treasures came from land now owned by the Province? Or might they have originated on land within an Inuit or Cree village? Isn't it true that the only thing we can say is that they came from somewhere within Quebec's borders?"

"And, we have to remember that once there were swept up by the ice, they could have been dropped off anywhere along the way, and that leads directly back to Placer Claims," Marie offered. "We're talking about placer deposits, found by definition in loose, unconsolidated material *on* rather than *in* the ground. I found mine in Maine, but surely there are more such deposits in Quebec. And I'm imagining somebody, some day, will turn up his or her own treasure in one of them."

"And you're thinking, what if a young Inuk or Cree, or perhaps an ordinary tourist, on a fishing trip or on the hunt for game, happens by pure chance to find a pile of nuggets like yours," Pierre said. "And, let's suppose, they are assayed and determined to be worth x dollars. Are you suggesting that that money should be shared, somehow?"

"However much that idea sounds like a pipe dream—no pun intended, yes, I am," Marie answered. "But only a small portion, say 5% or so, or at least some mutually agreeable and fair share, and further, I'm suggesting that one: such a thing could occur in Quebec as well as Maine; and two, it most likely would occur on land open to Placer Claims."

"For Pierre's and Louise's benefit, since you already told me, please share what you would do with that money," Dr. Parsons said, "And what if land where future treasures are found in Maine is privately owned, or part of a township, or otherwise restricted from mining? The same would be true of Quebec."

"On the second part of your question, I'm not sure, but perhaps the answer lies somewhere within Maine's Property or Real Estate Laws, and most likely would require input by the Federal Government. In Quebec's case, since 90% of the land is 'Crown Land' and controlled through Comprehensive Land Claim Agreements, some part of the Placer Claim procedures might require some tinkering, such as with a Rider, or some form of Amendment. I would defer to Louise for the answer to that question.

As to the first part: what would happen to the money, should there ever be any? Well, right now I'm thinking of something like a joint Trust Fund. I'd call it, 'The Ice Age Resources Trust,' the beneficiaries of which would include all aboriginals in Quebec and all members of

Maine's four, remaining Native American tribes.

Of course, at the moment, the money involved would be infinitesimal, since what we're talking about is known as 'alluvial mining.' Amateurs do the bulk of it, individually and informally. From what I've read, on a world-wide level, well over 90% of it is done in Africa, and it's dangerous, environmentally destructive, and extremely hard work. Some of it is done to finance rebel groups engaged in civil wars, which makes it very controversial.

Finds are rare, as I myself learned, but the key to the whole thing is location: knowing where to look. And, while it's prohibitively expensive on a large scale right now, I'm convinced that someday, somebody will develop the technology to better locate and extract nuggets like mine on a commercially viable basis. Then we'd be talking about a whole new ballgame."

Looking at his colleague, Pierre said, "I think we now have a better idea of where you're going with this. We're impressed, to say the least. One last question: you're implying that a lot of people and organizations, as well as the respective governments, would have to reach agreement on all this. How are you going to work that out?"

"Well, in Maine, there would be several players, beginning with the Federal Department of the Interior and the Bureau of Indian Affairs and the Bureau of Land Management. Then there's the Real Estate industry, the State Indian Tribal Commission, and of course, individual Tribal Representatives. Finally, there is a relatively new advocacy group based at the University of Maine called the Wabanaki Center. I'll defer to you, Pierre, as to knowing who would need to be involved in Quebec."

"Oh, goodness ... well, let me see ..." And, for the next few minutes, Pierre talked about the Inuit Tapiriit Kanatami, a 'national voice' for more than 55,000 Inuit in more than 50 communities, from Labrador to the Yukon. He also reviewed the role of the Makivik Corporation and the Kativik Regional Government of the Nunavik.

He went on to explain that while most Cree live west of Hudson Bay, there are close to 20,000 living in Quebec, 8,000 of whom live in the Nunavik. There is a Cree Regional Authority, which serves as an administrative body for the Cree Nation of Eeyou Istchee in Quebec.

Of course we'd also probably need the approval of Quebec's Department of Energy and Natural Resources as well as the involvement of legislative committees overseeing mining regulations and laws."

Dr. Parsons was quietly taking this all in, clearly enjoying the discussion and the interplay between her three guests. Finally, after a few moments of silence, she said, "Marie, the language in your grant proposal indicated you have about two years to accomplish your objective. After what you've learned this week, and particularly this evening, are you still convinced you can be successful?"

"I know it's not going to be an easy job, but, yes, I think I can, and in no small way thanks to you and your colleague's help and counsel. But, you perhaps know the old saying about retailing: 'location is everything,' I keep coming back to that. We know alluvial deposits can contain treasure, so the question remains: where are the alluvial deposits? I had one in my back yard. Where are all the others?"

Surprise Visitor

Marblehead Harbor, Massachusetts

On Thursday morning, a few days before his team's first scheduled meeting on the Quebec Project, Mel told Martha when she arrived that he would be leaving after lunch to catch up on his flying lessons at nearby Beverley Airport. He had logged close to 40 hours in the air, including 25 flying solo, and both he and his instructor felt he was close to being ready for his FAA check ride and private pilot licensing. All he needed was a couple more long cross-country flights. He was anxious to be able to fly on his own as a licensed pilot—especially between the firm's offices in Portland Maine and Quebec City. The plan for today was to make a round trip north to Old Town, Maine and back, which would add about four more hours to his log.

He was reviewing the report from Mark DeLyon when a call came in. A few moments later, Martha stepped to his door and said, "Are you available for a visitor?"

"Who is it?"

"She said her name is Webber, and that she was not far away. Sounded serious."

"Webber? Any idea what she wants?"

"She said she wants to talk with about your work, and she made a point of saying that she knows you." *Who could this be*, Mel thought to himself.

"Do you know where she is?"

"Yes. She said she's at the Coach House in Salem, on Lafayette Street. Said she could be here within the hour."

"Ok, tell her to get here as soon as she can. I have a little time before I need to get to the airport."

While he was waiting for the caller to arrive, Mel resumed reading the report, but immediately found his mind wandering. It was hard to concentrate. *Webber. Webber. Why is that name familiar? The only Webber I ever knew was someone I went to school with. Marie. Marie Webber. Wait! This couldn't possibly be her, could it? If it is, I wonder why she would track me down after all this time. Oh, well. Guess I'll just have to wait and see. Maybe she's looking for a job.*

Giving up on his reading, Mel glanced outside and noticed that the sky had lightened considerably. The weather was improving, just as the forecast had indicated it would. He had checked it before calling the airport to arrange for his flight, since he was restricted to flying only in good weather under visual flight rules. He was ready for a second cup of coffee and decided to take it outside for a short break before his visitor arrived.

Marie reached the Marblehead pier's parking lot and found a slot to park her car. When she looked toward the water, she immediately recognized her old friend Mel, standing at the edge of the dock, in front of his office with coffee in hand, apparently admiring the large collection of sail and powerboats arrayed from the harbor entrance to the town pier all the way to the shore of the Neck. She had not ever visited Marblehead before, although its maritime history and reputation as a sailing Mecca was well known to most New Englanders.

When she stepped from the parking lot onto the wooden planking, the sound of her heels caught Mel's attention, and he turned toward her as she approached. A broad smile appeared on his face as he recognized her. "Well, well, well. I'll be darned. If it isn't Marie Webber. From Moreville. How are you, Marie?" he said, giving her a polite hug.

"Hello, Mel," she replied. "Good to see you again after all this time. You're looking good. I'm fine, by the way, and thanks for asking." Glancing around the pier and harbor, she said, "Looks as if you're doing pretty well. I mean, fancy office on the water, in a famous, old village on the north shore." *What am I saying: he's one handsome dude, and this is the home of the mega rich! And the last time he saw me, I was a pregnant high school dropout ...*

"What's say we go into my office," Mel answered, grinning at her comments, "and have us a chat." Yeah, I guess I am doing pretty well, he thought. And you've turned out just fine yourself. You are one, good-looking lady. Better than I could have imagined. Can't wait to hear what you've done for yourself.

After going inside, Mel introduced Marie to Martha, using her full name, of course. When Marie was not looking, MOM flashed a wink and mimicked a silent wolf whistle to Mel as he and Marie were moving toward his office. *Hmmm, I guess MOM's impressed, too,* he said to himself and nodded in silent agreement.

Once they were settled, Mel asked, "So, Marie. Tell me why you came all this way to find me."

"Actually, I came from much further away than Moreville, or anywhere in Maine. I came from Wisconsin, where I've been living with my aunt Ellie ever since you and I last saw each other." And, for the next several minutes, Marie told Mel about the birth of her son, working on the farm, about her aunt's encouraging her to finish high school, and then how she went on to college and, later, earned her Law degree.

"I'm sure you remember that old place in Moreville where I grew up." *Oh, yes. I certainly do, and a certain mud puddle,* Mel recalled, thinking back with mixed feelings.

"I won't take time to give you all the details, but as it so happened, that property was left to me in a will and I was able to sell it." She recounted her son's discovery of the diamond nuggets. She also shared with him her recent visit to Ottawa, and the discussions she had there on her grant project.

"My goodness," he said. "You've been busy, and accomplished quite a lot for someone who grew up in a small Maine village. I'm impressed, to say the least, but you know, honestly, I guess I'm not surprised. I mean, the one thing I remember most about you is that you were always ahead of the rest of us. I have to tell you I was surprised to see you leave school so suddenly, although I figured it out ...

"You saw me in town that day, didn't you? When you were with your brother at the bank?" Marie said, quietly.

"Yeah, I did. Anyway, I can see now that you've been able to work things out, and for the better. I know you said you have a son. Husband?"

"No, working on my aunt's farm, raising my son, and going to school have kept me too busy for anything like that."

"This thing with the grant. It sounds like it's some challenge you've taken on. So, how did you happen to think of me, and how did you track me down?"

"Well, right after I closed on the Moreville property, I met this fellow DeLyon at the University of Maine." Mel was surprised by the coincidence, and did his best to maintain his composure, continuing to listen as Marie went on to relate how the Geology Instructor, while evaluating her diamonds, mentioned being in Quebec recently, working on a pipeline project with some guy named Mel.

"I didn't press him for details, except for how old this 'Mel' might be, and when he told me, I figured it had to be you. At the time, I didn't let on that you and I knew each other. So, I checked out your company's web site, and voilà, there you were. And here you are now."

"What else did Mark tell you about me?" Mel asked, mildly curious.

"Not a lot. He only shared a little bit about what you do, and where your main office was. He said you have others, too. It was only later, after my trip to Ottawa, I realized that you were someone I should talk to. And, I also now understand much better how Dr. DeLyon, as a Glacial Geologist, would be important to my project. It's actually something he's particularly well informed about."

"You of course would have no way of knowing this, but I'm seriously considering offering him a position with our firm."

"Are you? Good luck with that. He seemed pretty happy to me

with his job up there with the University."

"Yes, I know, and I'm not counting on his accepting an offer, but he would be a welcome addition to our team. I guess we'll just have to see how that turns out. Now, tell me more about why you think I can be of assistance."

Marie then went on to recount how, from her discussions in Ottawa, she came to appreciate the significance of locating alluvial deposits in Quebec. "From the little bit I've read about the work you do, and I'd sure like to hear more about it, you have to know quite a lot about ground conditions where you plan or build your pipelines. Am I correct?"

"Yes, indeed, and that's main reason why we hired Mark as a consultant to come with us on our first venture into our Quebec Project. We've been contracted to look into some routes being planned for up there, and we're just getting started. At some point, we'll need to pull together everything we can find on the geology of that Province. In fact, we'll be looking at a possible route from Quebec City to Portland at some point in the future. And, I'm planning another trip as part of the Project that will take me even further north, to an area called the Nunavut. You've heard of it?"

"Yes. We talked about it while I was in Ottawa. I haven't yet seen Quebec, or anyplace in Canada outside Ontario, but there were two people at our session in Ottawa who are natives of that Province, and I plan on catching up with them again on their home turf in Montreal. One is an expert on Constitutional Law, and the other specializes in Aboriginal Law. They both teach at McGill University."

"Interesting you should mention that," Mel said. "That University is a very familiar place. I, and others on our team, do seminars at McGill from time to time, at their Earth and Planetary Science Center. In fact, we held our first meeting for the Quebec Project right next door to the campus. And now that we are going to be working up there for the next several years, most likely we'll need some legal help from time to time. You have their contact information?"

"Sure. They're both terrific people, and I'm sure they would be a good resource for you. I'll drop them a note and let them know we've spoken."

"Good. And … Oh, I almost forgot, while I was at McGill, I ran across one of my former students. He's also happens to be a Geologist, and like Mark, his interest is in Glacial Geology. He would be an excellent source of information for you in your own project. I'll get you his name and phone number," Mark said. "He, too, has a bit of an interest in diamonds. Perhaps you should look him up, too."

"That's terrific, Mel," Marie said. "I need all the help I can get."

"So, you want to know about locating alluvial deposits. Well, I do have some information on that subject … just in, as it so happens, from one Mark DeLyon. It's considered proprietary at the moment, and it only covers a small portion of that enormous landmass, but I'll see if there's a way we can make it available to you.

And, if I had more time right now … I'm due at the airport for some flight time this afternoon … I'd love to go into more detail about our work in Quebec, and beyond, but … wait: what's your schedule like? What's next on your agenda? You like airplanes?"

"You fly?"

"Student pilot, at the moment, but I'm getting close to getting my license."

"I've only been up one time. My son and I flew from Wisconsin to Maine and back, but all my travel for this project so far has been on the ground. And, as to my agenda? I'm leaving here for another trip back to Maine, to the University, but this time to see the folks at the Wabanaki Center. I need to understand their role with respect to Maine's Native American tribes and, perhaps, the history of land claims in that State."

"Marie. I just had an idea. Will you be in Maine for a few days?"

"Yes, probably. Maybe even as long as a week. Why?"

"Because, as soon as I return to Marblehead, I'll be getting ready for a trip to the far north. Shouldn't take more than three days. So, how about this: you leave your car here, with MOM. Oh, that's Martha. We just call her that because she's Martha, our Office Manager. Since I'm going to Maine today, anyway, I'll fly you. You do your meeting and whatever else you need to get done there, and I'll come back for you whenever you're ready to return. I have a contact in Bangor I know who'll loan you some wheels for a few days. Then, when you're ready, we fly back here, and you'll be on your way. And we could start by having lunch on the way to the airport, and continue talking while we're in the air. Think you're up for it?"

"Whew, great offer, Mel. How can I refuse?" Marie said, quickly thinking it through. *This may turn out better than I could have imagined*, she thought to herself.

———

The flight to Old Town went smoothly, thanks to the good weather, light winds, and a near-cloudless sky. Mel explained that pilots described such conditions as 'severe clear.' After takeoff and climbing to his cruise altitude of 5,500 ft, Marie found herself surprisingly relaxed and comfortable in the plane's small cabin. The views seemed limitless, and in no time she was beginning to recognize landmarks, some of which Mel pointed out as they came into view.

She was wearing a headset that allowed her to not only hear Mel over the noise of the engine, but she could listen in as he periodically checked in by radio with people on the ground who were apparently tracking their flight.

"It's called flight-following," he explained, "And as long as the airports we'll be passing over have the time, they are courteous enough to monitor us on their radar and let us know if any other planes might conflict with our flight path. We get passed off from one airport to the other as we go along, and it's a wonderful service, especially for a student pilot."

They kept the conversation casual, and Mel was able to bring Marie up to date on his own education and experiences after high school. He also admitted that he was still single, and shared the story of his loss of Ms. Marquis. He also talked about where he had gone to school, and how he had started his business. Marie began to understand just how well Mel himself had done for himself, which, after thinking about it, came as no surprise to her.

After passing over Portland, Maine, he began to point out some ground features that he thought might be of interest to Marie.

"Marie, look off to your right, and you'll see a series of smaller mountains. Notice that the northern faces have more or less smooth slopes? And, you can see how the southern slopes are jagged and somewhat broken? That's a direct result of the ice shield that once moved across this area, sort of like a giant snowplow dragging over the landscape. And, if you drive to the top of Cadillac Mountain on Mt. Desert Island, you can see actual scaring in the rock where the ice dragged boulders across it on the way to the Atlantic.

They flew just west of the old Naval Airport in Brunswick and were passed off to Bangor International, and in no time, the big airport came into view. The tower controller directed Mel to pass directly overhead at 3,000 ft, watching carefully for any other traffic that might unexpectedly appear, and gave him the exact heading to Old Town. The landing pattern there happened to take them in over Indian Island, just to the north of the field, and Mel pointed that out to Marie.

She took in the scene as the reservation passed below, but kept her thoughts to herself. She still had very mixed feelings about it. After landing, and parking his plane at the Airport's FBO, Mel saw a pickup truck in the parking lot which he recognized.

Pointing to it, he said, "There's your ride, Marie. My friend came through, as he said he would. The keys should be in the glove box. You can probably just leave it here when I come back to pick you up. I have to see the folks inside to have my logbook signed, and then I need to be back in the air as soon as I can. You going to be ok from here?"

"Yes, Mel, and thank you so much for the taxi service. The trip was a pleasure. I can see now why you want your pilot's license. Great way to travel. It would have taken ... what? ... at least 5 hours on the road to get here?"

"Yeah, and the scenery is so much better from up there. And, of course, we were traveling in pretty much a straight line at close to 130 miles per hour over the ground. Well, good luck with your quest. I hope you get some more answers. Call me when you're ready for the return trip."

After a quick hug and a peck on the cheek from Mel, Marie took her small suitcase and walked to the pickup, which looked like an old beater on the outside, but on the inside she discovered it had a new interior and soon found out it had a new, powerful engine. *This thing has had some serious work done to it,* she mused, clearly pleased. After starting it up, the mellow rumble of the exhaust brought a smile. *I'd love to have this back on the farm, she thought. Aunt Ellie and Charlie would be thrilled.*

After getting a cup of coffee at the Dunkin Donuts' drive-thru, she headed for the Wabanaki Center's office on the University of Maine's campus.

The Wabanaki Center

University of Maine, Orono

Marie was able to find her way to the building where the Center was located quite easily, and was careful to find a parking spot well away from other vehicles—just in case ...

Reaching the third floor, she was greeted by a young student on a work-study program and shown to the office of Dr. Beth Harrison, Professor of Anthropology and Native American Studies. Her plan was to first establish contact, introduce the background for her project, and then seek as much information as she could acquire over the next two or three days to help her better understand how to pursue her quest.

"Good afternoon, Ms. Webber," Dr. Harrison said. "I received your letter of introduction and a copy of your grant project, and the only thing I can say is you have some challenge ahead of you. How can we help?"

"Let me start by telling you how this all came about," Marie began, continuing on for the next hour relating the details of her early years in Maine, her Native American heritage, her inheritance and sale of property as well as the treasures found on that land, and her decision to find a way to share her findings both with those on whose traditional lands they originated and where they ended up. What she was searching for was an organization that had good communication with the native tribes, and perhaps could assist in acquiring their support for her project.

"The river next to my property is part of the headwaters of the Penobscot River, and from everything I know, that region was home to the Penobscots for untold generations. The people I met a while ago over in the Geology Department said they are still finding relics and evidence of campsites on islands and in the gravel ridges along the river.

Now, as I understand it, most of the remaining members live on tribal land—the Indian Island Reservation, which they own outright and on which they govern their own affairs. What I don't know is how much additional land they own, how large it is, where it is, and how much land they claimed was theirs in the beginning—when the land claim treaties were signed back in ... when was it ... the18th Century?

"Yes, that's when it began, around the time of the American Revolution. Both the French and the British sought their support and worked out a variety of treaties. A short time later, but before Maine became a State, the US Congress passed the Trade and Non-Intercourse Act, designed to protect States and individuals from trading with Indians or buying their land without Federal approval. This, for the most part, was aimed at the western regions of the country, which were undergoing rapid expansion. In New England, Indian tribes were recognized only at the State level.

Meanwhile, the Massachusetts Bay Colony, apparently unaware of what Congress had done, was doing its best to promote white settlement in its northern territory and worked out a series of treaties with the Penobscot, and others, to claim the land for itself. The treaties were never ratified by Congress, as it turns out. And this omission was behind the recent passage of the Maine Indian Claims Settlement Act by the US Congress.

That legislation was prompted when Maine's Native Americans claimed ownership of something like 65% of the State's land, in which a third of the State's current population resided. Eventually, the tribes settled for full control over a few thousand acres and settlement payment of over 80 million dollars.

The Penobscots ended up with just over 4,000 acres, a trust account of some 26 million dollars, and Tribal control of a collection of islands in the Penobscot River. They then purchased an additional 150,000 acres of other, remote 'trust' parcels of State land with their share of the federal award. In the process, they became federally recognized sovereign Tribes. I should add that implementation—the business of self-government, control over their lands, and relationships with Federal, State and local governments, continues to be somewhat murky and, to this day, cause for endless debate and occasional lawsuits."

"I've read about some of that," Marie responded, "And, so, tell me: how many Penobscots are there?"

"Their population today is approximately 2,500, with another few hundred living within 50 miles of the Indian Island Reservation, but of course, at one time there were many more. When the first white settlers arrived in the 16th and 17th Centuries, it is estimated that there were more than 30,000 Native Americans living in northern New England. Within just a few years, however, 90% of them were dead from disease and malnutrition, and those remaining were steadily forced to abandon their nomadic ways and traditional style of living."

"I read somewhere that the Penobscot's defined their traditional territory to include all land within about 50 miles on either side of the Penobscot River and its tributaries. Is that right?"

"Yes, it is, broadly. Although there was another treaty made regarding land on the St. Georges' River to the south. As for the Penobscot River, the exchange would included land reaching nearly to the Canadian border in the western part of the State, to the east of Mt. Katahdin in the northeast area, not that far from the border, and all the way south to Frenchman's Bay near Mt. Desert Island on the coast. The Penobscot watershed is considerable, to say the least."

That last bit of information gave Marie and idea that she knew she would have to check out while she was here on the campus, but not today. And not here at the Center.

"Thanks, Dr. Harrison, that's most helpful. Now, please, tell me about the role the Center has with respect to the Tribes. I take it your location here on campus has something to do with it."

"Yes it does. As you may know, because this University is a Land Grant institution, Native Americans do not pay tuition or mandatory fees, and we coordinate the waiver program for tribal students. We also support teaching, research and publications in Native American studies. And, speaking of which, there are a couple of special events coming up, which we are sponsoring. The first is tomorrow evening here on campus, and the next one will be at the Abbe Museum in Bar Harbor the next day. Both will feature a special guest, Dr. Gerald Long-Feather, a Native American speaker, author and attorney. He'll be talking about Maine's land claims, which I'm sure you'll find instructive."

"Thank you. I think I'd better add at least one of them to my agenda, which is somewhat open at the moment. One final question: is the Center a-political? I mean, in the sense of promoting the interests of all of Maine's tribes? I know there is a Maine Indian Tribal-State Commission, and there is a relationship between the State and the Federal Department of the Interior's Bureau of Indian Affairs, but do you ever have occasion to propose, or actively support, legislation?"

"We are not political, at least not actively or publicly, but behind the scenes, we occasionally do research or undertake studies on issues relating to Maine's Native Americans that assist those involved in legislation."

"Ok, that's helpful. I may come back to you at some point when I have something more specific to research," Marie said, recognizing that her visit was coming to an end.

In parting, Dr. Harrison told Marie about other areas of the University that could offer assistance, such as the Anthropology, Sociology, and History Departments, each of which had faculty whose specialty related directly to Maine's Indians. "I'd be happy to send you their names, if you wish."

"Thanks, and thank you very much for your time today. This has been very helpful."

Marie drove to a nearby motel and reserved a room. Before

settling in for the night, she located a nearby family diner and enjoyed a quiet meal by herself. While there, she made a call home to chat with her son and aunt Ellie, telling them about her plane ride with Mel and bringing them up to date on her plans for the next few days.

Before leaving the campus, Marie had called the Geology Department and made an appointment to meet with Mark DeLyon again. He had classes in the morning, so she accepted his offer to meet him at his office just after lunch.

It was mid-morning the next day by the time she awoke, somewhat surprised at how tired she had been. After dressing, and organizing her materials, she stopped back at the same diner for a leisurely brunch. It was now just after the normal lunch hour, and she drove back to the campus.

"So, you're back," Mark said, smiling broadly as she entered his office. "You bring me some more diamonds?"

"No. I'm afraid that was it," she answered with an equally wide smile, remembering his analysis of the nuggets her son had discovered. "Since I was last here, and thanks to something you shared at the time, I was able to become reacquainted with Mel Johnson. Turns out we were once schoolmates, from the same town where my diamonds appeared. He actually flew me up here from an airport near his Marblehead office."

"You know, something told me you two knew each other." I thought she was far too casual about that 'oh, I knew somebody by that name ...'

"Yeah, we did," she replied, and told Mark a little about their being in school together, and about Mel working on a farm next to her property. "But, listen, the reason I'm here now is to learn more about the eskers you talked about earlier. You mentioned there are several of them here in the State. Do you happen to know where they are?"

"As a matter of fact, this Department is working on producing a map called the 'Ice Age Trail,' which will illustrate a number of glacial features that can be seen today."

Mark took out a map of Maine's rivers, and with a felt marker, showed Marie where some of those features, such as eskers and marine silt had been identified.

———————

"You see all those little reddish streaks? Those are eskers, and notice how they are laid down generally pointing north to south? That's more or less the same direction the ice shield took on its way to the Atlantic. And the shaded areas are where we've found large accumulations of marine sand and gravel, left-overs after the ice shield retreated. If kimberlite residue from Quebec was ever to be found, it would be in those eskers and marine silt," Mark explained.

"Yes! That's exactly what I've been looking for," Marie said, with more than a little excitement. "And, you know what? If you overlay a map of the Wabanaki Confederacy territory over it, they would all be included, but how about when I sketch in the traditional homelands of each of Maine's tribes? I wonder how many would be included."

Marie drew over the map Mark had used with a different colored marker. They both then stood back and looked at it more carefully.

"It appears there are a few eskers in the northern area in the lands of the Micmac and Maliseet, a few more in the eastern area in the land of the Passamaquoddy, and by far the largest number in the lands of the Penobscot," Mark said. "But, remember, we haven't finished our work on locating eskers. Many, especially in the north, are covered by timberland and not easy to find and map."

After a few minutes, Marie said, "There's an important Native American visitor in town who will be speaking here on campus tonight, and again tomorrow down on Mt. Desert Island. If you have some time, I could use your help in putting this information together in some kind of a summary. If I have the opportunity, I'd like to share it with him."

"Sure, I can make the time," Mark replied.

"He's going to be at the Abbe Museum in Bar Harbor tomorrow. When we were flying up here, Mel talked about some glacial evidence on the top of Cadillac Mountain, which I suspect you already know about. While I'm down there, I think I'll make it a point to drive up and see for myself."

"You should. It is impressive, and while you're on the Island, you might also visit the Jordan Pond House. The Pond in front of the gift shop and restaurant was created by the damming of a stream by glacial till, called a moraine. But the main reason to visit, and I've done it many times, is that they serve the most delicious popovers and gourmet teas you have ever tasted. If you have time, stop in and give yourself a real treat."

"I'll do it," Marie said, holding a copy of the map Mark had given her. "And, by the way, do you know of a map like this for Quebec?"

"Yes, although it's more technical, and you can get it through their Department of Energy and Natural Resources in Quebec City. You can find them on the web, although I understand the best source for information like that is through the Earth and Planetary Science Center at McGill. Mel has a connection there, and can probably ..."

"Yes, he mentioned meeting a former student from McGill who is into glacial geology. Roger something or other. Anyway, I have his name and contact information, someplace. Maybe I'll look him up. I plan on going to Montreal, anyway, at some point. I want to catch up with some people I met while I was in Ottawa. I've got a lot more to learn about Quebec."

Mark led Marie to a small conference room near his office and began working with her on her letter and maps. They made good progress, with Mark interrupting from time to time to refresh their coffee, or to retrieve additional reference materials, or to check with one of his lab assistants on some technical item.

During one of his absences from the room, Marie went to the ladies room and, on the way, happened to glance outside. To her surprise, finding that the sun had gone down and it was quite dark already, she realized that they had been working far longer than she had expected. And, a glance at her watch told her she was probably not going to make the first of the two talks by the Wabanaki Center's guest speaker. *Oh well, at least I can make the one tomorrow*, she thought.

———

Marie left town mid-morning of the next day and headed east on Route 1 toward the town of Ellsworth, a drive of about an hour and a half. About two thirds of the way there, after passing by the famous Lucerne Inn, she came to a point where a panoramic view of the coastal region opened ahead and well below her. She couldn't help but notice the array of small mountains that Mel had pointed out during their flight. The slopped northern sides and ragged southern sides were even more pronounced from ground level. It occurred to her that, now having learned a little about glacial geology, and spending time with Mel and Mark, it was as if she was seeing ordinary and familiar things on the Earth's surface for the first time.

Pausing for a lunch in one of Ellsworth's quaint cafes, she made her way to Route 3 and followed it all the way to the Island, home of Acadia National Park, the only fjord in America, and the summer estate of the Rockefeller family as well as an assortment of oversized estates owned by some of America's wealthiest families.

She followed the signs for the Park, picked up a guide-map from the Visitor's Center near the entrance gate, and headed for Cadillac Mountain. The guide noted that, although it was not generally allowed during the summer tourist season, visitors at the top of the Mountain at sunrise would be the first of anyone in the entire nation to see the sun on that day.

The winding road to the top ended at a large parking area, where Marie found a gift shop and public rest rooms. She inquired in the shop as to where to find the rocks with ice-age scars, and was directed to a trail that led her to a small, rocky field with a large, barren area of exposed, pink granite just below the peak. The grooves in the rock were easy to identify, and she was not surprised to notice that they were well lined up and pointed at the peak and on to the nearby Atlantic. *This whole Island is one, giant granite rock, and I can't imagine what it must have been like when that ice shield came along, dragging tons and tons of rocks over millions of years across this very ground I'm standing on, she thought.*

She spent several minutes enjoying the view, especially the one overlooking Frenchman's Bay and the irregular, rocky coastline for which Maine is so well known. Marie checked the time, and having some to spare, she decided to take Mark's advice and visit the Jordan Pond House and Gift Shop before going to the Museum.

She selected a small gift for Charlie and her aunt Ellie at the Shop, and then went to the restaurant, where she ordered tea and popovers. Given the choice of eating inside or outside, she chose the latter, and was directed outside to a wide lawn sloping downward to the Pond. There, she found a place at one of a number of oversized picnic tables arrayed on the lawn amid white birch trees, many surrounded by beds of wildflowers. She was immediately comfortable in this family-style setting, and promised herself that one day she would bring Charlie here.

A waiter brought her a pot of tea along with a porcelain cup and the first of her two popovers, just out of the oven. It was about the size of a softball, mostly hollow of course, and tasted … well, out of this world, especially with a dab of real butter and some locally made strawberry jam. Just as she was finishing her first, the second was delivered. *Mark knows what he's talking about. This place is spectacular!* As she was enjoying the last of her tea and looking at the Pond at the foot of the Mountain, she found herself thinking of Mel. *I wonder if he's ever been here?*

First Visit to the Far North

City of Iqaluit, Nunavut

Mel arranged for his trip to Nunavut through the office of the Minister of Economic Development and Transportation, located in the Inuit village of Iqaluit. Situated at the head of Frobisher Bay on the southeast coast of Baffin Island, Iqaluit's population was close to 7,000. The village's history reached back to the 16th Century, when first visited by an Englishman named Mark Frobisher, who was looking for an Arctic passage to China.

Seasonal trading posts in the 19th and early 20th Centuries, and the creation of a US Airbase, not unlike the one at Kuujjuaq in the Nunavik, during WWII, led to the gathering of a sufficient population to serve as a small town. With the signing of the Nunavut Land Claims Agreement, the residents of the Nunavut voted to establish their capitol in Iqaluit, and the population grew to its current level.

He originally had considered inviting Mark DeLyon to join him on the trip, but decided it wouldn't be necessary for this initial visit. He planned on being in Nunavut for two only days, and determined it would be premature and things were far too politically unsettled to undertake any ground explorations.

Mel's research into the subject of oil and natural gas reserves in the Arctic revealed that the Nuvavut territory may contain more than 300 billion barrels of oil, or a 5-year world supply, and something like 20% of the world's natural gas supply. To date, all recovery of such resources in the Arctic have been accomplished from a few land-based operations, and because so much of the Nunavut is made up of inland and coastal waters, which are iced-over the majority of the year, as well as a large assortment of remote islands with nearly impossible access, recovery had been severely delayed due to the exceptionally high cost and risks involved.

Roy Martin had asked Mel to explore the possibility of connecting potential sources of oil and natural gas in the eastern region of the Nunavut, to be collected by petroleum tankers and delivered to the head of the future pipeline infrastructure in the Nunavik in northern Quebec. The other matters to examine, of course, included the whole business of access and land rights-of-way, exploration and prospecting, governmental controls and approvals, transportation, and finally drilling rights. And, lastly, there was the matter of a deep-water port. Nunavut had none.

It appeared, for instance, that the entire area of Hudson Bay and its Islands as well as those in Ungava Bay, were now Nunavut territory. Within Hudson Bay, north of James Bay and close to the coastline of western Quebec, there is an archipelago of some 1,500 small islands (only one of which is populated by an Inuit community in the village of Sanikiluaq, population of 850).

The northern regions of Nunavut are also made up of a large collection of islands, one of which, named Axel Heiberg, is in a remote region known as the Sverdrup Basin in the Arctic Sea northeast of Alaska. It is estimated that this Basin may contain more than 335 million barrels of oil, which, if recovered, would have to be transported by ship south to Alaska and then pipelined south for processing.

At the eastern extremes of Nunavut, fronting the Davis Straits that separate Canada from Greenland, efforts are being made to conduct seismic testing for oil and natural gas, with serious opposition coming from the Inuit community fronting the Straits at Clyde River.

It was understood going in that this part of the project was going to be a long-term proposition, not without its controversies and challenges, but he knew his client felt it was important to gain an understanding of where things stood and to lay the groundwork for future planning efforts.

The trip began at oh-dark-thirty in Boston, with a one and a half hour long flight to Montreal that then connected with Canadian North Airlines for an eight hour long trip, non-stop to Iqaluit. Fortunately, the weather was excellent, and the views spectacular, especially watching as the green, forested areas of southern Quebec gave way to wide expanses of treeless and muddy-looking tundra, and then the open waters of the Labrador Straits as the approach was made to Baffin Island. And after about the first hour of the flight, there wasn't a road anywhere in sight!

During the final few minutes of the trip, the plane crossed over the Katannilik Territorial Park, famous for its waterfalls and wildlife. The pilot pointed out the Soper River that coursed through the Park and ran to the small Inuit village of Kimmirut off to the southwest. "Close to the where the river meets the sea near Kimmirut," he explained, "There is a waterfall that actually reverses course with each tide."

Passing directly over the village of Iqaluit at the head of Frobisher Bay, which had now become the Territorial capitol of Nunavut, the pilot brought the plane to a smooth landing at the local airport. MOM had arranged lodging for Mel at the Frobisher Inn hotel, and he arrived there after a short ride in a courtesy van, which was waiting for him at the terminal. He was somewhat surprised to find the amenities available at the Apex Hill facility included the 8-story hotel, a theater, retail shops, a nightclub and bar, and three restaurants—all with first class accommodations and reputations. The day had been long, and somewhat tiring, so Mel opted to have a light room-service meal and was in bed and asleep within an hour after arriving in Canada's largest and newest 'province.'

Following an absolutely wonderful breakfast at the hotel, Mel walked a short distance to Palaugaa Drive, on the other side of which he found the Court and Government Administration building and Mayor's Office, where he planned to make a courtesy call. He introduced himself to Mayor Susan Aabana and was invited to her inner office.

"Welcome to Iqaluit, Mr. Johnson," the Mayor opened. "We received a notice of your visit and will do our best to supply you with as much information as we are able during what I understand will be a brief stay in our village."

"Thank you, Madam Mayor," Mel replied. "As we indicated in our letter, we are a technical consulting firm in the employ of Quebec's Northpipe Corporation. Our work to date has been limited to advance planning for the transport of natural resources within and through Province of Quebec, but recent developments here in your province suggest we have much more to learn and incorporate in our findings and recommendations to our employer.

It will come as no surprise that the recovery of any oil and gas resources in Quebec Province is a long way off, perhaps decades, so our work up to this point is preliminary in nature. We are now doing our best to get a handle on what the future may hold for this province.

To begin, I am aware you have some history of oil extraction in your northern regions, specifically from the Sverdrup Basin on the Axel Heiberg Islands. And there are reports of a find of additional reserves in that same general area near Ellef Ringnes Island. Because of their remote location, it seems certain that any future recovery would be have to be transported by tankers to Alaska for processing to refineries, just as it was during the two decades of operation in the Sverdrup Basin.

I have learned that there is strong interest in conducting seismic testing to locate additional oil and natural gas reserves in the waters off your southern and eastern shores, in the Davis Straits and in Hudson Bay. As I'm sure you know, prior estimates have indicated there may well be considerable amounts there in the seabed.

That said, I am also aware that such testing is not without its controversy and is being challenged by a number of Nunavummiut, particularly those in the Clyde River area. I'm hoping to learn more about that from the Government's Minister of Economic Development and Transportation, whom I'll be meeting with this afternoon. As I see it at the moment, only recovery projects in this surrounding area would have implications for Quebec.

For example, if sometime in the future a pipeline infrastructure were developed for the Nunavik, oil and possibly natural gas recovered here in the Nunavut could be transported by ship and connect with that infrastructure for processing in Quebec City. Right now, of course, that is entirely speculative."

"Yes, I understand," the mayor replied, "By the way, Ms. Jan-Kanayuk and I had lunch yesterday, and she knows of your visit and is looking forward to meeting you.

"Well, that's good to know. Well, I've taken enough of your time this morning. Perhaps, before I go, you could take a few minutes to tell me something of your community here. I gather things are going well?"

"Yes, I am proud to report. Our resident population is approaching 7,000, and now that we have the Nunavut government headquartered in the City, our tourism business are continuing to grow and prosper. And, like yourself, we are seeing a number of visitors coming to this area in search of business opportunities. I'm certain you will be introduced during your visit with Minister Jan-Kanayuk to some of her people in the Minerals and Petroleum Resource Division.

I hope you can find the time during your short stay to visit one or two of our more popular attractions. I would encourage you to visit the Nunatta Sunakkutaangit Museum and gift shop, the St. Jude's Cathedral, and of course our Unikkaarvik Visitor Center. The staff there are very good at providing first-time visitors with a history of the area and our community, some examples of our local talent, and, of course, a variety of items that illustrate the true meaning of our culture and customs. I'm certain you will find it worth your while."

"I will make it my business to see them," Mel answered.

———————

Returning to the hotel for lunch, where he enjoyed a delicious arctic char wrap, Mel noted that the dinner menu included bison ribeye steak and decided he would give it a try later that evening. He had a little time before his next appointment, and traveled by taxi to see the St. Jude's Cathedral, referred locally as the Igloo Church. The white, rounded shape of the exterior resembled a traditional igloo, which made it a very impressive landmark. The church was the seat of the Anglican Diocese of the Arctic, covering an area larger than any other Diocese in the world. The church also served as a local parish church, with services conducted in both English and Inukitut.

Mel took a few photographs, some inside and several of the exterior, and then continued by taxi to the Visitor's Center, where he collected a few brochures and maps of the local area and the nearby Sylvia Grinnell Territorial Park Reserve, located some 5 kilometers away near the smaller village of Apex. Apex, he learned, was where all Inuit lived during the time the airport was used by the US military. He took a few minutes to admire and photograph a number of exhibits of Inuit life, arctic animals and sea creatures.

The Museum was only a few steps away in an adjacent building, which was formerly a Hudson Bay Trading Company store, and immediately upon entering felt as if he was visiting a scaled-down version of the Smithsonian Museum in the US Capitol. He took more photos of the exhibits of clothing, tools, and hand carving, as well as a number of colorful works by local artisans, and found his way to the gift shop. He selected a small painting of an Inuit on a seal hunt that he decided would look good in his office, several, small hand-carved figures as gifts for MOM, the other members of his team, and an arctic wolf-skin vest that he planned on wearing when he was back home and flying solo.

Almost as an afterthought, he purchased two more items: a necklace with a polished image of a narwhale made from walrus bone, for his new found friend Marie, and a miniature model of a sealskin kayak for her son, Charlie. He left the Museum and headed for his appointment at the Blue Inuksugait Plaza Building with a smile on his face.

The Abbe Museum

Outside Bar Harbor, Maine

Marie arrived at the Museum to find a small crowd of 50 people or so, gathered at the entrance. Minutes later, the doors were opened and she joined the others entering and moved on to a small meeting room off one side of the interior lobby. She found a seat near the front of the room, pleased that she had remembered to bring along a notepad. She also had a three-page letter that she had put together at the motel after learning of Dr. Long-Feather's visit.

Ten minutes later, a Museum's staff director appeared along with the guest speaker in tow and moved to the podium. She tapped the microphone, confirmed that the sound system was in order, and addressed the audience. "Ladies and Gentlemen, my name is Gilda Mitchell. Welcome to the Abbe Museum and thank you for attending this evening's program. As you may know, the Museum was founded in the 1920's, and is focused on Maine's Native American culture and history. Our exhibits contain over 50,000 objects created and used by the Wabanaki, from stone tools, to household items, to jewelry and musical instruments, representing more than 10,000 years of post-ice-age history here in this State. If you have not already done so, we would encourage you to visit the Museum during viewing hours to examine this marvelous collection.

Our guest speaker this evening is Dr. Gerald Long-Feather, a Native American speaker, author and attorney. He is here on a two-day visit from his home in Colorado, where he serves as a tribal judge for the Cheyenne tribe. Dr. Long-Feather teaches law at the University of Colorado, and is internationally known for providing valuable assistance to a number of tribes across North America in their quest for self-sufficiency, independence, and land rights. There will be a handout available for you as you leave, which will give you more information on Dr. Long-Feather's background and his numerous publications, letters, and addresses on topics of interest to all Native Americans.

And, now, please welcome Dr. Gerald Long-Feather, who will be speaking to us about the Maine Indian Land Claim Settlement Act."

Dr. Long-Feather was a man of about 60, tall, slim, with a full head of long, gray hair worn in a ponytail. He was dressed in a black, long sleeved dress shirt, dark gray trousers, and a brightly colored vest with embroidered figures and symbols representative of his home tribe. Black rimmed glasses served as a complement to his scholarly reputation.

He stepped to the podium, switched off the microphone, and walked to the front of the center aisle. He pulled out a nearby chair, turned it around to face his audience, and sat down. Spoken with a firm, deep voice that immediately demonstrated that amplification was unnecessary, he said, "I trust you will excuse my informality, but I always find it works better when exchanging ideas and information on complex or sometimes difficult topics.

Now, as a first time visitor to this State, you should know that I am aware that people like myself are described as 'from away.' Perhaps, however, you'll appreciate that the people whom I'll be meeting with tomorrow—from the Passamaquody and Penobscot tribes, might have a somewhat different take on that label."

That brought a few chuckles from those in attendance as well as a smattering of applause, and it was clear that he had put everyone at ease. For the next several minutes, Dr. Long-Feather gave a summary of his background, some of his recent work with a number of tribes, both in the US and in Canada, and his special interest and experiences in dealing with Indian Land Claims.

"I'm not sure how many of you know this, but for a good portion of the last half of the 20th Century, the policy of the United States Government was to terminate all Indians—as Indians. Yes, many laws and policies were enacted with the aim of 'civilizing' Indians and assimilating them into the mainstream of society, ending special relationships between tribes and Congress—and, of course, any further financial obligations and support by the US government. As one well-known Native American Senator said at the time, what you seem to be saying is: 'If you can't change them, absorb them until they simply disappear.'

Shortly after the end of WWII, with the support of a larger and more rational segment of that same Congress, an Indian Claims Commission was created, whose purpose was to hear historic claims of Indian tribes against the US. As might be expected, land was the dominant concern. The Commission was not permitted to grant or restore lands, however, and could only provide monetary awards based on the value of the lands lost. By the time it completed its work, two and a half decades later, the Commission's awards totaled nearly one billion dollars.

To the surprise of many who had no knowledge of the conditions under which far too many Native Americans were living, as they had for generations—with extreme poverty, high rates of unemployment, struggles over the lack of health care, basic education, and wholly inadequate housing, those funds were put to good use. To their credit, they were able to reach beyond their reservations and play a role in the economic development of their states and this nation in a number of areas, such as wind farms, a bottled water plant, real estate, construction, and energy.

Today, there are over 400 casinos owned and operated by over 200 tribes, and I recently learned of plans by some tribes to become involved in defense contracting. Here in Maine, the Passamaquoddy's tribe of nearly 800 members on their Pleasant Point reservation and another 600 living close by, hoped to be able to open a casino themselves. A vote for approval, however, did not pass, so I'm informed. Reports suggest they haven't given up on this plan, and in the meanwhile are moving ahead on other ventures. As I'm sure you know, they happen to be located in one of the State's most impoverished counties, and they are now focused on projects designed to provide jobs and, as a result, give a boost to their own as well as the region's economy.

Any formal granting of land rights was accomplished either through judicial or by Congressional action. That is what happened here in Maine, when a suit brought by the Passamaquody and Penobscot tribes resulted in the passage of the Maine Indian Land Claims Settlement Act, signed by President Jimmy Carter, and I'll talk more about that in a few minutes.

Incidentally, the Commission's work also generated the publishing of more than 200 books, containing some but not all the materials covered during the course of their hearings. As you might guess, I have spent a good part of my career reviewing these books.

Another outcome of the Commission's work was the granting of federal recognition to a number of tribes, predominately in the western States, but also including those in this State. This immediately opened previously denied access to a wide variety of federal services and programs to the tribal communities. And, you'll be happy to know that today there are more than 560 federally recognized tribes in this nation, all of whom now share a set of basic rights.

I turn now to the business of land claims and tribal sovereignty. First, you should understand that the recognition of Indian tribes by the federal government implied 'sovereignty,' and business conducted between 'sovereigns' is routinely done on a government-to-government basis. This custom, of course, immediately raised the question of the proper role for States and administration of state and municipal laws on tribal lands and within Indian reservations, with a potentially significant impact on the practice of self-rule and self-governance.

As a case in point, part of the monetary award given for lost land by the Commission here in Maine was reserved as Trust Fund monies, which the tribes were free to utilize for the purchase additional lands or investment properties outside the reservation—with the approval of the US Congress, of course. Additionally, the interest earned on a one million dollar investment of those same Trust Funds for each tribe was earmarked to assist tribal members over the age of 60.

Prior to my trip here to Maine, I learned that the tribes did acquire timberland in some remote areas, as well as invest in the ownership of some businesses. Some of these ventures were not successful, but most were, and one or two have apparently returned handsomely on that investment. I expect I'll be hearing a lot more about this tomorrow when I meet with tribal members."

At that point, a member of the audience stood up, was recognized, and related the story of the Passamaquoddy's purchase of a New England's only cement manufacturing plant, a long-standing and well recognized business, overseeing improvements to its operation, and selling it five years later for over three times the original purchase price.

Another person talked about the attempts by one tribe to establish a spring-water bottling plant as well as a commercial maple syrup production facility on tribe-owned land.

When Dr. Long-Feather resumed, he said, "You have alluded to another bone of contention, and the primary reason I was invited to make this visit, which has to do with Tribal-State relations. To say that those relations are strained would be an understatement. For instance, there is a history of tribal members being elected to serve in the Maine State legislature, where they serve — and continue to serve, without voting privileges.

And, after the Settlement Act was passed, Maine closed its Department of Indian Affairs and replaced it with a Tribal-State Commission, an advisory group tasked with implementing the Act and serving as the primary communications vehicle between the State and the tribes.

Now, the Settlement Act granted municipal status to the tribes, which they interpreted to mean giving them access to State and County funds for things like road maintenance, for example, since the tribes make annual payments to the State in lieu of taxes. They viewed it as distinct from and in addition to their sovereign status. The State, however, argues that their municipal status replaces their sovereign status, which they apparently refuse to recognize.

This leads to the final area of concern—legal jurisdiction, or the rights of the tribes to establish tribal courts to oversee minor civil and criminal crime committed by Native Americans on their lands. And, by extension, they seek tribal control over matters such as wildlife management and environmental protection activities. There have been a number of recent news accounts here in the local media about this, and I understand there are several cases presently being worked through the State and federal court systems.

Whether it's the area of land claims, or preserving traditional customs and languages, economic self-sufficiency and political self-governance, what is important to note is there has been considerable progress made in recent decades by Native Americans to contribute to economic improvements while continuing efforts to reclaim their traditional way of life and preserve their thousands-of-year-old culture.

In conclusion, it is fair to say that much remains to be done, and my hope is that I will be able to gain a better understanding of some of the unresolved issues during my brief visit and, in the spirit of cooperation, provide some advice and guidance to both the policy makers and tribal leaders.

If any of you have questions, I will be happy to answer them as best I can. And, thank you for coming here this evening."

For the next several minutes as the audience began to disperse, Dr. Long-Feather patiently answered questions by the few individuals who stayed behind.

Marie was the last to approach, and after introducing herself, said, "Thank you, sir. That was very interesting, and I'm impressed that you spoke without notes. I am engaged in a project under a research grant that concerns a good portion of the tribal lands you will be visiting tomorrow, and I have prepared some information I'd like to give you.

Your comments about the ability of the tribes to acquire

investment property beyond their reservations got my attention, primarily because of the way it relates directly to what I'm attempting to accomplish. I hope we can find time, later, to pursue this more in depth, perhaps after we've returned to our homes. I know your stay will be short, so I've written a summary which, I hope, will be easy to digest."

As she handed over her materials, she said, "The letter includes my biography and a brief description of a project, along with a couple of maps. If, after reading it, you agree it has merit, I'm hoping you might find it worthy of discussion with the tribal leadership during your visit tomorrow. My intent is to follow up personally at a later date, when I have a more fully developed proposal ready.

I grew up about an hour north of the Penobscot reservation close to the Penobscot River watershed, although my home is currently in Wisconsin. Well, I won't take more of your time now, but I thank you in advance for your interest. I have included my contact information."

"I will do as you ask," Dr. Long-Feather replied, handing Marie a business card while accepting her materials and placing them in his briefcase. "So, you are saying this matter should be of interest to the Penobscots and the Passamaquoddys?"

"Yes, as well as the Maliseets and the Mic'macs. All the Wabanaki, in fact, in this State."

"Well, now you have my attention," Dr. Long-Feather said. "I'll make it my business to review your materials before my next meetings."

"Thank you, sir. I couldn't ask for more."

When Marie returned to the lobby on her way to her truck, she paused for a moment to look around at some of the window displays. *Someday, if and when I get to bring Charlie here for popovers at the Jordan Pond House, we'll have to come back and visit this place, too.*

Visit to Government Headquarters

City of Iqaluit, Nunavut

Mel found his way to the recently constructed Nunavut Government headquarters building in the Blue Inuksugait Plaza Building after a short ride in a local taxi. He used the directory in the lobby to find his way to the offices of the Minerals and Petroleum Resource Division on the second floor. After a short wait, he was shown to Minister Jan-Kanayuk's office.

The recently elected Deputy Premier and Minister was a mature, pleasant woman of about 60, dressed in a bright blue dress. She wore what looked to be handcrafted silver earrings and matching necklace, depicting iconic images from her native background. She and her family were long-time residents of Iqaluit, and she had served in a number of government and public service agencies before being elected to serve as Minister.

"Good afternoon, Minister," Mel began. "I'm pleased that you are able to find time to meet with me. My name is Mel Johnson, and I am here on a preliminary visit to learn what I can about this community and the government of Nunavut."

"Welcome, Mr. Johnson," the Minister replied. "And, please, you may call me Ms. Jan, as most everyone else here does. As you may know, our government is relatively new, and we are proud to say that we are a 'public government,' representing the residents of some 28 communities here in the Nunavut.

You might also be aware that this government is still evolving, and a good deal of our time is spent on devolution matters. I must say, progress is mixed, but there will come a day when we will become a full-fledged territorial government, having earned our right to full self-control over policies that best serve our lands and resources, our waters and, most importantly, our residents—almost 90% of whom are native Inuit.

I did receive your letter of introduction and have a general idea of your interests, and in that regard, I have arranged for you to spend some time with one of our Senior Advisors, Mr. Mike Soluk. Until things change, and we sincerely hope they will in time, the Crown has retained the right to control and decide on all matters relating to the recovery and transport of oil and natural gas resources. Mr. Soluk is well versed on all current operations, and I'm sure will be an important resource for you and your clients down the road."

"Thank you, Min … Ms. Jan," Mel said. "As we noted in our letter, we are fully aware that at this point, any planning work we do has to be considered speculative."

"Yes, I understand, Mr. Johnson, and may I also say that your coming to us this far in advance of the start of any operations is a welcome and most satisfying act on your part. While the Land Claim Agreement that created us includes a number of provisions requiring joint consultation between outside operators and private investors and our government, our history includes, sadly, far too many instances of our being either informed and involved after-the-fact, or not at all when it comes to the exploitation of our many non-renewable resources.

You may go on, now, and meet with Mr. Soluk. I'm sure he will brief me later on your discussions. And, again, Mr. Johnson, thank you for visiting and welcome to the Nunavut."

One of the Minister's administrative aides escorted Mel to the opposite end of the building, where was shown to Mr. Soluk's office. Mike Soluk, like his boss, was also native to the Nunavut, born and raised in Baker Lake. He had come from a family of miners, and had earned a degree in mining engineering from Queen's University in

Kingston, Ontario.

Soluk was a tall man of about 45 years of age, wearing a dress shirt and dress slacks, over which he wore a bright vest decorated in arctic graphics. If you didn't know him, you might say he was a high school teacher, or perhaps a lawyer.

"Good afternoon, Mr. Johnson. Ms. Jan said you'd be coming. How may I be of service?" Soluk said with a smile.

For the next several minutes, Mel went over the reason for his visit and what he hoped to learn about the current state of affairs regarding Nunavut's natural resources.

"Well, why don't we begin by taking a look at a map that I utilize on a daily basis."

―――――――

Soluk began, "You first have to appreciate that the area you are looking at is the size of Western Europe. It is rather large, to say the least. We have a handful of roadways, all relatively short and usable only during the summer season, and none extending beyond our border. A road in the south to connect with the Province of Manitoba is in the planning stages, but it presently does not enjoy great support.

The area in the far west, known as the Kitikmeot Region, contains the largest concentration of active mines, and it, too, is where a great deal of activity to locate and identify additional minerals is occurring today. There is an iron mine at the northern end of this Island—Baffin, and there are a few more mines in the central-southern region.

As to oil and natural gas, it turns out that considerable reserves have been located in our far northern regions. There was, in fact, an operation that produced oil for more than a decade near Ellef Rignes Island on the Arctic Ocean. That oil was shipped to Alaska for processing.

And based on the latest information available, there may be as much as 350 billion barrels of oil reserves and 20 trillion cubic feet of natural gas beneath our islands and in our seabed. And that only opens another whole can of worms, because while we have something like 75,000 square miles of territorial waters – much of it internal and populated with islands which are next to impossible to access, and thus it would be prohibitively expensive to support recovery operations, especially in today's world market. And, that's not to mention environmental concerns, such as spill containment and cleanup.

In our more southern regions, such as Hudson Bay, Ungava Bay, and the Davis Straits, where some testing has already been completed and more planned, there are also promising signs of substantial reserves of oil and natural gas. I expect it is this area that is of most interest to you and your clients."

"That's correct, Mr. Soluk. I think the best way to explain it is this: we are just beginning to take a look at future pipeline routes through and within Quebec Province. The sources of oil and or natural gas for such pipeline infrastructure are, at this point, only partially identified, and limited to those presently originating in Canada's western Provinces.

Our clients have asked us to explore the possibility of developing routes to Quebec City storage and refining facilities from northern Quebec, or more properly, the Nunavik. The thinking behind their efforts focuses on future extraction sites within Quebec's maritime limits, or more precisely, from the seabed surrounding that Province. But there seems to be some question about those limits.

What is the official boundary between your territory and the Nunavik and Quebec proper."

———

Soluk replied, "The Nunavut boundaries originate from 1912 and are based on the original boundaries for the Northwest Territories. Those boundaries were incorporated in the Nunavut Land Claim Agreement under which we were established as a separate region. Under those terms, the Nunavut extends throughout the Hudson and

Ungava Bay regions to Quebec's shoreline.

We learned recently that the definition of 'shoreline' is apparently being disputed, since the Agreement failed to specify whether that means the low tide or high tide line. In any event, it appears that Quebec and the Nuavik have no 'seabed' in the way that term is understood.

There have also been some objections raised by the Canadian government, the Province of Quebec, and the leadership of the Nunavik about all this. The first issue is the Inuit community of Sanikiluaq on the Belcher Islands in Hudson Bay. Although the residents Sanikiluaq have been supported by the former government of the Northwest Territories for many years, there are many people in that community who are closely aligned with the residents of Kuujjuarapik on the Nunavik mainland near the mouth of the Great Whale River. In other words, they would prefer to be associated with the other Inuit villages in the Nunavik.[5]

We learned recently that the definition of 'shoreline' is apparently being disputed, since the Agreement failed to specify whether that means the low tide or high tide line. In any event, it appears that Quebec and the Nuavik have no 'seabed' in the way that term is understood.

There have also been some objections raised by the Canadian government, the Province of Quebec, and the leadership of the Nunavik about all this. The first issue is the Inuit community of Sanikiluaq on the Belcher Islands in Hudson Bay. Although the residents Sanikiluaq have been supported by the former government of the Northwest Territories for many years, there are many people in that community who are closely aligned with the residents of Kuujjuarapik on the Nunavik mainland near the mouth of the Great Whale River. In other words, they would prefer to be associated with the other Inuit villages in the Nunavik.

---

5   Quebec is not the only province with this jurisdictional issue. The federal govern-ment delineated the borders for Manitoba and Ontario in the same year, and their borders also exclude the water. This means in all three provinces, the borders shift daily, from high to low tide, and they're also shifting with climate change. http://www.cbc.ca/

And that brings up a second issue -- a deepwater port, which the Provincial government of Quebec hopes to develop as part of its economic development plan, which they call Plan Nord. The potential conflict here is self-evident, since deep channel access would be within Hudson Bay.

And, finally, there are some islands in the southern sector of James Bay that fall within the Nunavut boundary but which were not included in the Land Claims Settlement. The Cree from that area who have used the islands for centuries as part of their hunting and fishing grounds asked for and were recently given the 'right of ownership' by the Nunavut government, although that action may yet end up in a court of law.

In fact, there are some of us here who see the possibility of this entire matter of maritime boundaries being raised to a higher level, re-examined under International Law and the UN Convention on the Law of the Sea. Under that Convention, a nation's maritime border includes a territorial sea, which extends 12 nautical miles from a territorial baseline, or shoreline at low tide. Then there is an exclusive economic zone extending 200 miles from that same baseline. If the maritime limits were to be revised for Quebec, the Nunavik, and the Nunavut, it would have serious implications for the economic future of all of them."

Mel said, "Of course, for the present, this is all moot, is it not? I mean, the Crown government has reserved the right to control all non-renewable resources here in the Nunavut, and the same applies to the Nunavik by the Provincial government of Quebec. That is, until and unless devolution is completed and the territorial governments are granted those rights."

"I would have to agree," Soluk replied. "And, I suppose that leaves you with several open questions."

"It sure does," Mel said. "First, let's start with the assumption that your southern maritime territory in Hudson Bay, the Davis Straits, part of the Hudson Straits, an Ungava Bay are shown to contain and become locations for the extraction of oil and natural gas resources from the seabed. And, you'd have to take into account the local and important objections being raised by the indigenous communities to testing and exploration activities. That issue would have to be resolved.

But, let's suppose, eventually, those resources are tested and proven and that same area, under the control of the Nunavut government, is developed through agreements with the private sector.

Just as occurred a few years ago in your northern extremes, where oil was extracted for a decade or so, arctic products have to be transported by ship somewhere for processing and refinement – Alaska, in that case. So, too, would the oil or natural gas recovered in your southern waters have to be transported by ship to storage and refining facilities in, say, Quebec City.

This is made a little more difficult because you don't have a deepwater port and no large-scale storage facility, at present. And, neither does the Nunavik, with the exception of a deep sea wharf in Deception Bay used by the Raglan Nickel Mine. Until the question of maritime boundaries is resolved, I suspect there would be little interest in the development of pipeline infrastructure in the Nunavik and Quebec to transport a product that's not their own.

And, lastly, there is the matter of operating drilling platforms in arctic waters. The experiences so far have shown this to be problematic, considering safety and environmental concerns, and of course the effects of extreme weather conditions as well as the high costs involved. It appears that arctic drilling sites have to be constructed on some kind of landmass, either real or man-made, and close enough to a mainland to facilitate temporary storage.

So, any recommendation to proceed with plans for pipeline routing in the Nunavik will depend on how these questions are eventually answered. That's how I see it at the moment. How about you? I have the feeling everything I've just said is something you already know, and know well."

"You're correct, Mr. Johnson," Soluk replied with a smile. "We're doing our best to stay on top of things."

"You know," Mel began, pointing to the map, "There is one

other possibility to consider. Let's suppose for a minute that the Nunavik and Ontario and Manitoba are granted rights to their own Exclusive Economic Zone. That would include the eastern and part of the western shore of Hudson Bay, Ungava Bay, and a portion of the Hudson Straits – probably out to the midline.

And, let's suppose that any oil and gas recovered within that zone is transported south by pipeline rather than by a ship, which I believe could be economically justified. And, yes, I'm aware that the shipping season in these parts is limited to about 6 to 8 months of the year, with some help from icebreakers, of course.

Now, let's say that you, too, recover oil and gas within the Nunavut's Zone, here in the southern regions. And, rather than shipping that product all the way to Quebec City, you were to take advantage of the Nunavik's nearby pipeline system and, perhaps under some type of cooperative arrangement, utilize it as a means of transport, to everyone's advantage."

Mike Soluk considered this for a few moments, and said, "Accepting that for the present, this is all hypothetical, you just might have something there. I'll share your ideas with my colleagues and see what they think, with your permission, of course."

"Please do," Mel replied. "And let me know what you decide. I'd like to incorporate our discussion in my report to my client."

"I'll be happy to do that," Soluk replied.

"Thank you, and thank you for your time today. I'll be leaving first thing in the morning, but right now, I'm looking forward to enjoying my first taste of bison rib eye back at the hotel. If you're free, perhaps you'll join me?"

"You're going to love it, and thank you for the offer, but I promised my daughters I would come to their school this evening and watch them perform a new set of tribal dances they learned from their grandmother," Mike Soluk said.

"I understand. Then maybe on my next visit. The offer stands."

Visit to Montreal

McGill University, Montreal

Mel landed just before noon at the Old Town Airport and taxied to an area next to the parking lot where Marie was waiting. She had returned the truck to its original spot and, along with a thank you note, a full tank of fuel, and a small gift of a box of fresh strawberries, left it fplauor the owner to retrieve. She had already dropped off the key at the base operator's office.

The trip back to Mel's airport in Massachusetts went well, and the two of them spent much of the time during the flight bringing each other up to date on their recent visits. Mel was wearing his new arctic fox vest, which Marie decided made him look like a true outdoorsman—and quite the handsome dude. She was also pleased with his choice of gifts for her and her son Charlie.

"Charlie's going to love his new toy, and this is beautiful, Mel," she said, admiring her new necklace, "And I appreciate that you thought of us. I mean, now we'll be able to say we have something from the other end of the earth ... or, at least from what you described. That place sounds intriguing."

"It is," Mel replied. "And, only someone who has actually visited there can appreciate just how remote and unique it is."

They returned to Mel's Marblehead office. Marie planned to return to Wisconsin, and Mel would be spending the next several days working on a report for his client. As they were parting, there was a tender moment when Marie was thanking him for flying her to Maine and giving her his support for her project, and he was thanking her for finding him again after such a long absence, and they embraced. Both found the moment to be a little awkward, especially when it ended with a long and gentle kiss.

"Marie, I ... wow, that was nice," Mel said with a smile, and a bit lost for words.

"Yeah, for me, too," Marie answered, quietly.

More than two months later, back at the farm, after Marie had shared what she had learned with her aunt Ellie and was watching Charlie play with his new toy kayak, she was updating her files on her trip to Maine.

A letter had come from Dr. Long-Feather, and she was pleased to learn that he had shared her materials with the tribal leaders. They apparently were taking seriously her idea of purchasing any available lands, which contained eskers, and most were well informed of the locations of commercial gravel pits to the north.

She began making plans for her trip to Montreal, when thoughts of her time with Mel arose once again—and not for the first time. *Ok, there's something really nice that could be happening here that I don't fully understand, and I sure hope it can continue, but right now I'd better get my mind back on business …*

She contacted Pierre and Louise at their McGill University offices and arranged to meet with them. Both had recently completed their Fellowships in Ottawa and returned to their faculty positions in Quebec. Louise offered her home as a place to stay, which Marie gratefully accepted. For this trip, she decided to fly.

A few days later, she arrived at Montreal's Pierre Elliott Trudeau

International Airport after a four-hour trip with a brief stopover in Detroit. Louise Pelletier was at the airport to greet her, and the two of them traveled to Louise's home in the Le Plateau Mont Royale section, often referred to as the Plateau, only a few blocks south of the University.

After putting her things in a guest room, Marie returned to the kitchen, where she met Louise's fiancée Hubert Monfort, a third-year resident at McGill's School of Medicine, who had just arrived after his work at the nearby Royal Victoria Hospital. Following introductions, the three of them settled in a small living-dining area with a glass of chardonnay from a local winery, accompanied by a serving of Le Cendre de Lune, or Ash Moon, cheese.

"Hmmm," Marie said following a taste of the appetizer, "I have to say this is every bit as nice as anything I've tried from my home state of Wisconsin, which prides itself on its cheeses."

"Well, thank you," Louise replied. "Hubert found it in a shop just down the street. By the way, I hope you like seafood. We're having almond-crusted trout for dinner. I'm trying one of my mother's favorite recipes."

"Sounds good to me," Marie answered with a smile.

"So, Louise has told me a little about your project. Tell us, how is it coming along?" Hubert asked.

And for the next hour or so, with Louise periodically retreating to the cooking area to check on her dinner preparations, Marie related her experiences and findings from her Maine trip. She showed them copies of some of her maps, particularly those dealing with esker locations and traditional tribal lands of Maine's Native Americans.

When she told them about becoming reacquainted with Mel Johnson, she mentioned that he had referred to another faculty member at McGill, and asked where she might find him.

"His name is Dr. Roger Gagnon, and he's supposed to be quite an authority on Quebec's glacial geology."

"I can look him up," Louise said, and went to retrieve a directory from her home office. When she returned, she handed Marie a note pad on which she had written his phone number and address. "He's at the Earth and Planetary Center,"

"I think I'll give him a call in the morning and see if he might have some time to meet with us. Mel said he's very well informed on glacial geology, and the little amount of time I spent with Mark DeLyon at the University of Maine's geology department suggests Dr. Gagnon could be important to help us understand the landscape here in Quebec," Marie said.

"This Mel fellow. You say you and he grew up in the same town?" Hubert asked.

"Yes, we were schoolmates when we were young. He owns his own consulting firm, which specializes in energy transport—oil and gas pipelines, and I would say he's been very successful at what he does. You know, in fact, he told me he and others on his team are invited to conduct seminars here at McGill from time to time. You both may have passed right by him on your way to work, without knowing who he is, of course. He's working on a petroleum project right now that is based in northern Quebec, although from what little I know about it, there is some question as to who might actually have the rights to recover the resources."

"There are stories in the news quite frequently about that," Louise said. "Just the other day, in fact, I watched an interesting discussion about devolution and its potential impact on economic development in the Nunavik and Nunavut regions. My faculty colleagues and I are guessing that the progress is being slowed by the unresolved maritime boundary question."

Marie said, "Mel also mentioned that. He said it has a direct bearing on his own work, and that the Crown government is reluctant to let go of the reins on that one."

"Yes, indeed. We talk a lot about it at work. But while it is interesting, it's not exactly germane to what you're working on, is it?" Louise suggested.

"No, you're right," Marie said. "When you and Pierre and I last talked, you said you might be taking another look at the Mining Act and mining regulations."

At that point, sensing the turn in topics and how serious the discussion was about to become, Hubert spoke up and said, "How about this, ladies: Let's defer any more business chatter until you and Louise and Pierre get together tomorrow. I'm starving. What's say we enjoy some of Louise's special culinary talents. I am pleased to say, Marie, that she's very good at it."

The meal was delicious, as promised, and for the rest of the evening, there was no more discussion of Marie's project.

Hubert had the day off, and was sleeping in. While he was enjoying his well-deserved rest, Marie and Louise shared a breakfast of coffee, croissant with cream cheese, and a cup of fresh fruit. They left for Louise's office, and along the way, Marie again complimented her host on the lovely dinner she had prepared the night before.

"You know, if you ever decide to give up teaching, you might consider opening your own gourmet restaurant. That trout was out of this world!"

"Well, thank you, Marie. I do so love trying new things in the kitchen."

————————

Louise had a light schedule—only a mid-afternoon seminar to conduct, and was free until then. Marie called Dr. Gagnon, and he had some spare time and agreed to join them at the Law Center. While she was on the phone, Louise left the office and almost immediately returned with her colleague Pierre in tow.

They gathered in a small conference room next to Louise's office. Roger soon arrived and was immediately invited to talk about his work, and his background. It was then that he and Louise discovered they had grown up in the same city—Mt. Laurier, although they had never met before. Louise was, though, familiar with his mother's B&B.

"Mel spoke highly of you, Roger" she said. "I remember that he said that you were one of his 'students.' Thank you for helping us out today. We really need your expertise."

"Glad to lend a hand," Roger replied. "I first met Mel when I was an undergraduate. He and others on his team occasionally visited the center to offer two-day seminars on topical subjects, and I took one or two of his. It was good meeting him, again, not long ago, in fact."

"Yes, he told me about that. He and I go back quite a ways, too," she added with a smile.

After a short break to get coffee, the four of them took a seat around a table, ready to begin the discussion of Marie's project. She gave each a copy of her grant proposal, and began by reminding everyone that the whole idea arose the discovery of some diamond nuggets on her property—nuggets that were contained in an esker, and had been previously handled by a Penobscot, one of Maine's Native Americans.

Pierre began, "Marie, you mentioned you were there recently, and had a chance to learn more about them and their land."

"Yes. I was able to get a handle on the scope of their traditional homelands, as well as land they now own, and I have a couple of maps that show where particular glacial features overlap with those lands," she said. She shared the maps with the others at the table, and went over her visits to the Wabanaki Center and the Abbe Museum. She also shared her meeting with Dr. Long-Feather.

Roger said, "I see you have a surficial geology map, Marie. From the University of Maine?"

"Yes, and the geologist there, Dr. Mark DeLyon, was most helpful in identifying the location of eskers, moraines and the like. He, by the way, was the guy who confirmed that my 'diamonds' were really diamonds. I also asked him if he knew of a similar map for Quebec, and he suggested that your department, Roger, would be the best place to make such an inquiry."

"I may have what you're looking for. One of my students gave me this map just the other day, and although the study area covers only a portion of the Province, it does indicate that we, too, have a significant number of eskers that have been identified," Roger replied. "And, there is a search on to find more.

You know, you mentioned that your diamonds came from the alluvial till in an esker. Well, that's not the only place they can be found." And, he went on to tell the story of his having found diamondiferous materials along the highway near his home in Mt. Laurier while doing a ground survey as an undergraduate student.

You know, you mentioned that your diamonds came from the alluvial till in an esker. Well, that's not the only place they can be found." And, he went on to tell the story of his having found diamondiferous materials along the highway near his home in Mt. Laurier while doing a ground survey as an undergraduate student.

"Mel and I had a chance to talk about that very thing, when he was here last," Roger continued. "There is a lot of glacial till around that area, particularly to the north." He referred to his map and pointed to the Gouin Reservoir and the Lac Albanel region.

"This will be a big help," Marie said. "May I use it in my final report?"

"You certainly may," Roger replied. "Just make sure it is properly cited.

——————

For the next couple of hours, the discussion ranged from topics such as how diamonds are formed, how they get to the surface, what happens to their host rock afterward as the earth warms and freezes, and on to how they are transported by the dynamics of the ice shield. Roger was especially helpful on the technical details.

They then turned to the subject of locating diamonds, from their origin in lode sources such as kimberlites in Quebec and the Nunavik, to their destination in eskers, moraines and other types of debris fields—both in Quebec and in Maine. Louise introduced the subject of lode and placer mining, noting that Marie's diamonds would be considered alluvial, placer objects. "I was able to do some homework after our first meeting, Marie, and came up with some interesting facts about mining in Canada.

First of all, there are more than 60 different minerals and metals produced in this nation. And, on a world scale, we are first in the mining of potash, second in uranium and cobalt, third in aluminum and tungsten, fourth in platinum, sulphur and titanium, and fifth in nickel and diamonds. Recent surveys show there are nearly a half million people in Canada engaged in the mining and mineral processing industries. And, incidentally, more aboriginals are employed in that sector than any other in all of Canada."

"What about alluvial mining, on a commercial level?" Marie asked.

"There is some of that going on, but it is for gold, not diamonds," Louise answered.

Pierre spoke up, saying, "Marie, what has me intrigued is your idea for sharing a portion of the value of any diamonds only found outside the boundaries of lode claims, such as the Renard Mine operation. Why not include them as well?"

"Lode claims, as I understand them, imply exclusivity to any diamonds recovered within the claim boundary. And, they are usually large-scale, expensive, and complex operations. To suggest the operator of such a mine, after the fact, would be willing to agree to reserve even a token amount of their profits for a trust fund for aboriginals is not realistic in my view. Whether or not the concept could be applied to any new claims and operations is another question. What do you think, Louise?" Marie asked.

We'd have to take a look at the mining laws," she replied. "And that approach may be feasible, but perhaps it should be reserved for a later time. I say that because, as I understand it, you are focusing on alluvial deposits, and that would be covered under placer claims."

"I'm no expert on mining laws," Roger said, "But I'd have to agree with Louise. I mean, those diamonds of yours were in a placer deposit."

"Ok," Marie said. "So, let's think of it this way. We know placer deposits can be found over most of both regions—Quebec and Maine, and some deposit locations, such as eskers and moraines and alluvial fans, are known and have been mapped. We also know that any diamonds found in any of those deposits originated in Quebec.

If we go back to the beginnings of human occupation following the end of the ice age, or about 12,000 years, we might think of the aboriginals at both ends of the distribution 'trail' as the rightful 'owners'—or, more accurately, 'custodians' of the land and everything it contained. Any such ownership claims have been transformed historically through treaties and land claim agreements, and are now incorporated in the federal, state and provincial laws and regulations relating to land use."

"So, you are suggesting that a kind of homage be paid to that original, aboriginal custodianship? Is that what you are really saying?" Pierre asked.

Before she answered, Roger said, "I unearthed diamondiferous materials along a Canadian highway, and you found some from an esker in Maine. Both were transported from an unidentified origin in Quebec, but both were found in historically aboriginal lands."

"Precisely. That's why I refer to my diamonds as 'ice age treasures,'" Marie said. "What I am trying to envision is a legal mechanism that would incorporate a find by an individual—just as in my case, on privately owned property, to a find by an individual or mining company, on leased, public land. By public, I mean state-owned, as would be the case in Maine, or Crown-owned, as in Canada."

Louise then said, "And, of course, you would exclude any land on which a mining claim of any kind already exists, I presume. Or, are you thinking of excluding lode only claims?"

After a few moments of thought, Marie replied, "Well, we are focusing on placer deposits, so, yes, at least for the time being, let's defer on the subject of lode mining."

"Alright, let's project ahead, and say some curious and enterprising individual gets himself—or, herself—a few simple tools, studies up on the basics of how to identify diamond-bearing rocks, and goes exploring in a gravel ridge or perhaps an esker. It is all rather informal, and largely amateurish, but is that not prospecting, and would any kind of permit be required?" Roger asked.

Louise referred to a document called the Mining Act of Quebec and read, "It says 'to prospect' ... and I'm paraphrasing here ... is to seek mineral substances while neither owning the land nor having mining rights—which I take to mean a mining claim—on the land. It also says surface substances would include 'every mineral substance that is found in its natural state as a loose deposit.'"

"There is also a provision that requires taking into account the 'rights and interests of Native communities,' and there is language here that makes it abundantly clear that, with few exceptions, all mineral substances belong to the Crown, while at the same time, there is language that promises a 'fair share' of any wealth generated to the Province."

"It says that a permit, good for five years, is required for prospecting on any land. And then it goes into extensive detail as to the conditions and locations where prospecting is permitted, and where it is not. I understand there is a map of this, somewhere. Do you know of it, Roger?"

"Give me a few minutes. I know someone in our department who may have one," he said, and left the room to retrieve the information from his colleague.

When Roger returned, he passed out copies of two maps. The first showed the areas of Quebec where mining is prohibited, with the reasons noted. The second, from his personal office records, illustrated the known kimberlite locations as well as the known lineaments, or underlying surface faults in the Province. These fault lines, he explained, are prime areas for concentrations of mineral deposits as well as underground water courses.

After everyone had taken a short break and returned to the conference room, it was Pierre who asked, "Marie, I recall your having talked about a trust fund, which I believe you said was to benefit all aboriginals in Maine and Quebec. My question is: what kind of mechanism would be used to get money into such a fund?"

"There are two scenarios, and here's what I'm envisioning from my own case: when my diamonds were found, they were simply rocks. After they were confirmed as diamonds, I had them assayed by a jeweler, who determined their monetary value. If I had decided to sell them, or cash them in, if you will, I would see the buyer—in this case, the jeweler, paying me 95% of the full value. He would then submit the remaining 5% to the trust fund. That is, if he were required to by law.

As an alternative, I would receive the full 100%, and I, as the 'seller,' would pay my 5% to the trust fund."

"That seems feasible, I suppose, for any similar case of what we might label as 'informal' mineral recovery, by individuals, operating in an area where prospecting is permitted. Now, imagine this occurring on a larger, more organized, commercial scale. There would still be a 'seller' and a 'buyer.' The question then is: how could we legally require the 'buyer' or the 'seller' to hold back and then contribute that 5% to your trust fund?" Pierre asked.

Roger took this in, and then said, "You know, there is one other factor that may need to be considered. Those nuggets of yours, Marie, were evaluated as rough, uncut and unfinished, diamonds. Just as with commercially mined rough diamonds, they, too, have a market value as raw minerals. Converted to polished gemstones, or processed into diamond-surfaced tools or polishing devices, their retail value would substantially increase. So, I might suggest you keep it simple, and focus on only the proceeds of the first sale made after they are recovered as rough diamonds."

Louise said, "That's a good thought, Roger. And, if we were to limit the responsibility of contributing to the trust fund to the owner, or seller—immediately after recovery, we would avoid having to deal with non-local buyers and processers, or any subsequent re-sale activity in retail markets. That keeps the focus on the actual location of any discoveries—here in Quebec, or in Maine. And, we can sharpen that focus by limiting ourselves to diamonds, although there is a good deal of activity in placer mining for gold."

The group suddenly realized they had been working so intently that lunch hour had come and gone. They agreed that they had done all they could for the moment, and that they would reconvene again in two days. Marie offered to put together a draft of a proposal, incorporating the materials and information they had just discussed. She ended the meeting by thanking everyone for their help.

———

Louise and Hubert left for work early the next morning, leaving Marie alone in their home and free of any distractions as she began to organize her draft. She decided to use a resolution template, which she began with the title 'Sharing Ice Age Treasures.' An hour and a half later, she examined what she had written, which read:

Whereas;

The lands of the Province of Quebec and the State of Maine were overrun and their surfaces substantially altered by glacial ice shields in at least four, major southward advances beginning some 500 million years ago;

Volcanic kimberlites (bearers of diamond minerals) on and above the surface in Quebec were disassembled by the mechanical forces of that ice and redistributed through glacial transport and alluvial (water-born) means within Quebec and across the common border with Maine, from the Nunavik to the Atlantic;

Following the last advance, ending some 12,000 years ago, those same lands have been occupied by aboriginals (the (Cree and Inuit in Quebec, and Wabanaki (Penobscot, Passamaquoddy, Maliseet and Mic'mac in Maine);

Beginning in the 16th Century, with the arrival of European settlers, those native populations were depleted through disease and other forms of mistreatment, with those remaining forced to abandon most of their traditional homeland, their nomadic lifestyles, and many of their traditions and customs;

The presence of important natural, non-renewable resources on those lands, has motivated the respective Federal, Provincial, and State governments to encourage the economic development of those resources, acquiring land control through treaties and, more recently,

Comprehensive Land Claim Agreements;

The Agreements incorporate and codify the rights and interests of aboriginal communities and tribes at the Constitutional level, including the protection of wildlife habitat and surrounding environment, respect for the preservation of native languages and cultural traditions, and support for health care, housing, education, employment and economic welfare; and

A growing number of Agreements regarding the recovery of natural resources, particularly in Nunavik (the Inuit region of northern Quebec) include the requirement to contribute a 'fair share' of the wealth received from such recovery operations to the affected native communities; now, therefore

Be it Resolved

That any alluvial placer deposits containing mineral diamonds located in the Province of Quebec or the State of Maine, on (a) lands formerly recognized as aboriginal territory (i.e., prior to the passage of any Comprehensive Land Claim Agreement), (b) all public lands currently under Provincial or State control, to include all lands open to permitted prospecting, or (c) any privately owned land on which permission to prospect is granted by the owner, be recognized as unique Ice Age Treasures;

That any individual (or business entity) recovering such diamonds (or diamondiferous material), and sells or trades them for their monetary value, be required to contribute at the time of sale a portion equal to 5% of said value to an Ice Age Treasures Trust Fund;

That the Quebec Mining Act (for the Province in general), the Sanarrutik Agreement (regarding mining in the Nunavik region), and mining laws and regulations for the State of Maine, be amended to recognize and incorporate the above in it's mining laws, statues, and regulations; and

That all contributions to the Ice Age Treasures Trust Fund be maintained, controlled, and monitored by a Board of Directors, with annually rotating self-elected Chairmanship, and whose members include: (for Quebec) an appointee from the Government of Canada, the Government of Quebec Province, the Grand Council of the Crees, and the Makivik Corporation; and (for the United States), an appointee from the US Department of the Interior's Indian Affairs Bureau, an appointee from Maine Indian Tribal and State Commission, and an appointee representing each of Maine's four tribes; and

That all monies in the Fund be distributed annually, in equal amounts on both sides of their common border, to all aboriginal communities in Quebec and Maine.

Marie read her draft document through one more time, and after several minutes, decided she had done all she could for the time being, feeling somewhat like the sculptor who produces a beautiful carving by taking away everything from a larger, blank stone that doesn't belong.

Having never visited Montreal before, and having some time to spare, she decided to take advantage of her freedom spend the afternoon exploring the historic sites of nearby Old Montreal district and visit the world-renowned subterranean mall. In their earlier talk of foods, Louise had mentioned that there were a number of well-known restaurants in the area. Before leaving the house, she called Louise and invited her to be Marie's guests for dinner—along with Hubert, of course, if he was free.

"You're choice of restaurants, since I'm a stranger in your city."

"Thank you very much. I'm sure Hubert will be pleased, too. A friend told me of one I might suggest. It's called the Barroco, with a French-Spanish cuisine, and she said their braised duck was to die for. How about we meet there at 6. It's on St. Paul Quest."

"See you there," Marie said.

The dinner was spectacular, and the evening was most enjoyable. They managed to keep the conversation pleasant and light, with much discussion of fine dining in Montreal, some quirks of Canadian law, the burdens and occasional fun of a medical resident, and only the briefest mention of Marie's project, when she said, "I did finish a first draft for our next meeting."

———

The next afternoon, Marie, Louise, Pierre, and Roger met once again in the Law School's conference room, and immediately began to study the Marie's document. After several minutes, they began to offer comments, the first by Pierre. "For the life of me, I can't seem to find anything missing, and you've done a remarkable job of covering all the 't's' and 'dotted 'i's.' What does strike me, however, is whether or not any aboriginal, either in Quebec or in Maine, will ever see a dime. That is, presuming you are able to convince the appropriate authorities to accept it and enact it into law."

Roger replied, "Well, I agree, she's covered all the bases, but you should know that in fact there is a fair amount of prospecting going on here in the Province. And, then, there's folks like your friend Mel, who is about to do some rather extensive ground sampling for his pipelines.

And, from what I've read, there is a good deal of gemstone prospecting going on in Maine, aimed largely at the tourist population and local school children. Remember, too, that we're talking now about individuals and small groups, working in gravel pits and along ridges, with simple tools. As Marie mentioned, there are many signs pointing to placer mining of alluvial deposits becoming a commercial enterprise, and that may well be where the real money is. "

"And, didn't you already say you're prepared to make the first contribution? From your own diamonds? Marie?" Louise said.

Marie laughed, and answered, "I did, didn't I. Yes, if I cashed them in, I'm told I could get almost a thousand dollars. Of course, there would first have to be a Trust Fund where I could make my $50 deposit."

To which Pierre replied, "And, then it would need to be authorized and approved and overseen, and all that. Marie, how in the world are you ever going to get this adopted into law? The odds are, it won't be easy."

"I'm thinking I might just have to start from the top with a visit to my congressional representative—and maybe a Senator or two.

Hopefully, they'll know how things get done in Washington. As for Canada, I'm planning a return visit to Ottawa, where I'm hoping Dr. Michelle Parsons will have some ideas—and maybe come connections in the Canadian Parliament.

Eventually, I would want to include some discussions with the Maine tribal community, and of course, the native communities and representatives here in Quebec. After all, they would be the beneficiaries, of the Trust Fund—which doesn't yet exist, and which contains no money at the moment, and is funded through the sale of alluvial diamonds which are yet to be found."

"And, all of which is carried out under non-existent laws and regulations," Louise replied.

Several moments later, looking at each of her friends in turn, Marie smiled and said, "You know, if my son hadn't found those diamonds on my property, this whole thing could easily sound like a pipe dream. I guess now, the job will be to see if I can make it real. I've got a year and a half remaining on my grant, so wish me luck."

After a pause, she added, "One of my favorite authors, the late Maya Angelou, once said: 'Tolerance of the inadequate is possible only through ignorance of the alternative.' I'll just keep believing. That's what I'll do."

Return to the Farm

Outside Madison, Wisconsin

A year had passed, and Marie efforts were finally beginning to show signs of progress. She had organized her materials—the Resolution, supporting maps, and a half-dozen reports on mining laws, aboriginal histories and tribal rights, and land claim agreements—into a bound Report and made two dozen copies. She had also done a good deal of traveling, mostly by herself and some in Mel's company, over the course of the past year.

On her first trip, to the nation's Capital, she had met with and provided copies of her Report to her congressional representatives in Washington, D.C.; to an Undersecretary in the Interior Department's Bureau of Indian Affairs; and, in Maine, to the current head of Maine's Indian and State Tribal Commission.

While in Maine, she also revisited the Wabanaki Center and spent a day with the Chiefs of the Penobscots and Passamaquoddy Tribes. It pleased her to learn that both Tribes understood and appreciated what she was attempting to do, and had followed her advice—actively supported by Dr. Long-Feather—to acquire ownership of new properties where alluvial till had been identified. And, she made time to visit again with Mark DeLyon, who had actively support the effort by providing the Tribes with student volunteers from his department. The students were offering training, and conducting field trips for young tribal students to areas where alluvial till was prevalent and where prospecting was permitted.

In Canada, she had returned to the University of Ottawa and reconnected with Michelle Parsons. Through that connection, she was introduced to the Minister of Natural Resources, and through him, to a Deputy Minister overseeing the Geological Survey Department. There, she was shown a series of maps, including several that more clearly identified the types of glacial features that she was focusing on.

Both the Minister and his Deputy expressed interest in Marie's Report and the inherent proposition it contained regarding improved relations between the Crown and its indigenous populations. In fact, the Deputy Minister suggested that he would give it further study to determine whether or not the concept might be expanded from the Quebec-Maine area to other Provinces across southern Canada having common borders with US States with Native American Tribes.

While she immediately saw the merit in the idea, it also increased likelihood that a lot more time would be required before it was ever implemented. Nonetheless, she was grateful for the reception she received, and left the Parliament campus on a positive note.

While Mel's project was proceeding in halting stages due primarily to the unresolved matter of maritime boundaries and control over arctic oil and natural gas resources, as well as the slow pace of devolution in both the Nunavik and Nunavut regions, he continued to make periodic trips to the area. His focus was now on pipeline routing down the western regions of Quebec.

On their first trip together, Marie flew to Montreal, where the two of them met and traveled on to the James Bay area on Creebec Airlines. Mel was wearing his now favorite wolf-skin vest, while Marie was dressed in dress slacks, lightweight sweater, and her usual leather jacket. They landed in the small, Cree village of Nemaska on the shores of Lac Champion, the official headquarters of the Grand Council of the Crees. The Grand Council had offices in Montreal, but Marie was advised to take her proposal to the highest level of decision makers in their home village.

They might have driven, but the trip from Montreal, through

Mt Laurier, was almost 900 miles, the last portion of which would have been on the very remote and unpaved James Bay Highway. Mel was anxious to share his client's possible plans for future pipeline development, and Marie was, of course, looking to share and gain support for her Ice Age Treasurers project. The entire area was rich in alluvial deposits, and to the north, in the village of Kuujjuarapik on Hudson Bay's eastern shore, a new deep-water port and petroleum and natural gas storage facility was still in the works.

A meeting had been pre-arranged with the Director of Land and Sustainable Development, Robert Tanoush, who spent an entire afternoon discussing their separate projects. While the reception to Mel's plans were politely heard, with most of the interest seeming to focus on employment opportunities for native populations in the region, he had come away with the sense that running pipelines through traditional homelands was not going to be a popular venture.

On the other hand, Marie's project was received with enthusiasm, and seen as a way of further associating the Cree, especially younger Clan members, with their native lands. The day's visit culminated in a wonderfully prepared native meal of slow-roasted goose at the lakeshore's Nemaska Motel and Restaurant, where they had overnight reservations—in adjoining rooms—at least for this trip. Following their meal, they gently held each other's hand while enjoying a glass of sherry in front of the Motel's fireplace, and each, at some point, admitted later to having given more than a little thought to altering their decision on room arrangements.

Mel arranged for a charter flight the next day from Nemaska north to Kuujjuaq, where they had arranged to visit with officials of the Makivik Corporation, located near the village center on Naalavvik Street, and the Kativik Regional Government, located a short distance away on Kaivivvik Circle, both of whom were heavily involved with the 14 Inuit communities in the Nunavik.

For Mel, it was a return to an area he and Mark DeLyon had visited more than a year earlier, and he was looking forward to being brought up to date on local views regarding devolution and the unresolved issue of maritime boundaries. Marie was immediately struck by the size of the community, and the extent of modernization on display in an otherwise remote and wild region. Mel had mentioned that Kuujjuaq was the largest of the dozen Inuit villages in the Nunavik,

Makivik was created at the time the Nunavik Inuit Land Claim Agreement was signed into law for northern Quebec. The Corporation was given responsibility to distribute compensation funds, and serve as an intermediary agency between the Federal, Provincial, and Native governments and communities. Over time, it had increasingly focused on economic development and job creation for Intuits, participating in contract negotiations and managing and distributing funds generated through mining and hydroelectric projects. It also operated Inuit Airlines, which provided regularly scheduled flights from Montreal and Quebec City to Inuit village airports throughout the Nunavik.

The Kativik Regional Government, formed at nearly the same time, was focused on community development and public services. They worked closely with each other, and Mel and Marie concluded it would be important to establish a relationship with both organizations.

It was no surprise, then, that the reception they received was nearly identical to that experienced earlier in Nemaska. Both groups listened politely to Mel's presentation on the development of future pipelines and the recovery of oil and natural gas resources, seizing again on the inherent promise of new employment and training opportunities, but there was no arguing that the concept was going to be a hard sell—and for understandable reasons.

Marie's Report, on the other hand, was greeted with enthusiasm, and a display of interest much like that shown by the Cree government's representatives. As she distributed her maps highlighting the possible locations of glacial deposits and till in the area, many of those in the room began pointing to locations and adding comments such as 'my uncle traps beaver there' and 'we make our annual caribou hunt right in that area.'

Before going to their lodging at the Auberge Kuujjuaq Inn near the airport, where they would stay before returning to Montreal, Mel decided to pay a visit to the Outfitters where he and Mark had arranged their trip to the Torngat Mountains.

"Ms. Tukkiapik is not here at present," Mel was told by a young man at the service counter, "Trish said she plans to return after her baby is born. She married a young pilot with Inuit Air, not long after you were last here, Mr. Johnson."

"Well, please give her our best," Mel said. As they were riding to the Inn, Mel told Marie about the trip he and Mark had made to the fjords and wild rivers of the Torngat area beyond Kangiqsualujjuaq.

"If you think this village is remote, you could not begin to imagine just how far off the grid that place is. I'll show you some photos sometime."

When they reached the Inn, one of two B&B's in the village, and approached the check-in desk, Marie took Mel's hand and said, "You know, Mel, we've known each other for a long time, and I've kind of enjoyed this business of traveling together. I'm ready to dispense with this 'adjoining room' routine. How about you?"

"I couldn't agree more," Mel replied, smiling broadly.

———————

The next morning, while waiting for their breakfast to be served, with the sun lighting the room and the faces of its few guests, Mel quietly removed a small box from his vest pocket and handed it to Marie.

"I don't have to tell you that I'm a pretty happy fellow, right now, because I've been found by someone whom I've not only always liked but have come to love. I'm asking you to be my wife, Marie—if you'll have me."

Marie opened the box to reveal a beautiful, diamond engagement ring.

"Mel," she said, "It's absolutely gorgeous, and, yes, I'll marry you."

After a long kiss, Mel added, "I almost knew you would say

yes. After all, your talent for making good things happen whenever diamonds appear is unmatched."

Marie laughed and said, "I'll need a little time to talk this through with aunt Ellie and Charlie before … you weren't thinking of a specific date, were you?"

"No, it's all right. Take some time. I'd like to get to know your son. And, your aunt Ellie. And, the farm. And, you've got your project to finish, and I'll be traveling a lot more in the next months … so, we can work it out later."

"Good. That sounds like a plan. A very good plan."

————————

Several more months passed, and in response to her repeated follow-up calls and letters, Marie continued to feel encouraged to think that, one day, and hopefully sooner than later, action would be taken by the powers that be on both sides of the border, to bring her project to fruition. She made her final report to the Robert Wood Johnson Foundation, thanking them for their support and promised she would continue the work on her own.

Postscript

The Farm outside Madison, Wisconsin

Charlie's 12th birthday was just days away. He was outside in the yard, playing with his dog Fred after being cooped up inside for three days of unrelenting rain. Marie and her aunt Ellie were in the kitchen, cleaning up the breakfast dishes, when Ellie happened to glance outside. She saw Charlie waving and pointing to the long driveway leading to the highway. Someone was approaching in what looked like an old, beat up truck. She didn't recognize it, but when Marie stepped next to her and saw the vehicle, she let out a gasp and covered her mouth with her hands.

"Oh, my God!" she said, knowing immediately who it was.

A few minutes later, Mel stepped into the yard next to the pickup, enthusiastically greeted by Fred. Charlie stood back, his attention shifting between the stranger and his mother and aunt, now standing on the front porch behind him. Marie, of course, was smiling broadly, and said, "Hi, Mel. That is my son, Charlie. That's Fred, his dog. And, this is my aunt Ellie."

"Hi, Charlie … Ellie. I should probably explain," Mel said, looking at Charlie. "When your mother was visiting in Maine a while back, she got to drive this truck, and really liked it. Well, it belonged to a friend of mine, and since he has four more just like it, he was willing to part with it."

Looking around at the farm and surrounding fields, he said,

"It needs a new home, and this looks like a pretty good place to me. Of course, it also will need a new driver, but since you're not quite old enough yet, maybe your Mom's aunt Ellie should be the one doing that for a while." As he looked back at the pickup, he noticed that Fred was giving it a good sniff. "Oops," he said, as he watched the dog pee on one of the rear tires, "I see that your dog is giving it his sign of approval."

Marie leaned closer to her aunt and said, quietly, "You are not going to believe what's under the hood. And under what looks like a lot of rust is one mean, almost new, machine."

Ellie replied, also quietly, "I'll take that truck, because I'm pretty sure you'll be keeping the driver."

"Yes. I. Will. Yes, indeed. Sakes alive."

Birth of a Diamond

It starts three billion years ago when you are 145 miles below the Moho (*Mohorovicic discontinuity*) layer, or boundary between the rapidly cooling rocky crust and the molten mantle of the new planet Earth. You are roiling about in bubbles of liquid magma, two-thirds of the way down into the upper mantle, in a 200-mile-deep region known as the lithosphere, or the crust and uppermost mantle taken together. Many millions of years earlier, partial melting and convective forces have caused you to drift upward out of the hot soup surrounding the inner core.

The pressure on you is nearly 750 tons per square inch, and the temperature is more than 2,500 degrees Fahrenheit. In one fugacious moment you crystallize into a harzburgitic diamond (*from the Greek adamas, or unbreakable*), made of pure, inorganic carbon. As you grow, your unique structure becomes a repetitive pattern of extremely strong covalent bonding of 4 atoms, forming a face-centered cubic, or diamond lattice. Because of your rigidity, you are nearly impervious to contamination, and for the next two billion years, you continue growing.

Close by but in very different conditions, crystals of garnet and green pyroxene (*eclogite rocks*) and crystals of olivine, orthopyroxene and clinopyroxene (*peridotite rocks*) aggregate and cluster together, while other crystals of pure carbon, your equal in every way, experience unexpected changes in pressure and temperature and cease their crystalline growth, reverting to mundane graphite.

Meanwhile, above you, the surface of the Earth's crust continues to be bombarded by asteroids, comets, and interstellar meteorites—resulting in the appearance of diamond 'cousins.' Some cosmic bodies bring with them already created carbonado diamonds, with a similar crystalline structure. Other cosmic objects strike carbon-rich areas of the Earth's hardening surface, instantaneously creating impact microdiamonds and nanodiamonds, with yet another kind of crystalline structure.

At some point during the course of the next three hundred million years, in the company of other crystalline clusters you are moved to a point below a fault (*weakening or separation*) in some of the oldest, thickest and coolest area of the crust. You are steadily being elevated by magmatic pressure, and then, suddenly, you are thrust upward into cracks and fissures leading toward the surface. Now you find yourself contained in a steadily cooling vertical pipe of igneous rock. Most of the magma carrying you is blown outward in a volcanic larval eruption, but you remain behind within a now solid kimberlite pipe (*maar*) in the volcano's mountainous core.

There you remain for millions of more years, during which time the Earth cools to an extreme, reaching a point where the entire surface is covered in a layer of snow and ice. You wait out five major cycles of thawing and re-freezing, much of the time buried under a moving ice shield thickened to many miles in depth and producing mechanical forces beyond imagination that alter the surface landscape surrounding you.

In time, the rim of the mountainous volcano where you now survive, along with the remaining pipe in which you are contained, is crushed by the massive forces of the ice shield down to nearly surface level. The rim and its core is ground up into pieces—some as small as sand grains, and others dwarfing the largest known bull Mastodon, and then swept up into, onto, and under the ice, and carried off by the wind, melt-water rivers, and streams.

You are bounced around within your softball-sized host rock, until at some point you come to rest within a gravel ridge adjacent to a nearby riverbed. The ice shield that delivered you soon recedes and the land around you dries as melting increases in a steadily warming Earth. The eclogite and peridotite rocks holding you in place erode by the natural forces of wind and rain, and eventually you are released to become a free-standing nugget.

Thousands of years later, long after the ice shield has fully retreated and the transformed lands are now occupied by the first hunters, you are discovered. An unusual 'stone' to the eye, perhaps, and at best a curiosity piece, but you are in fact a diamond. And after another few thousand years, someone decides you are valuable.

USA *Today* News Item from October 13, 2016

Many people spend hours digging for diamonds at the Crater of Diamonds State Park in Arkansas only to walk away empty-handed. But that wasn't the case for Dan Frederick, of Renton, Wash., and his daughter Lauren, who found a 2.03 carat diamond less than an hour after they arrived at the diamond site on Oct. 3.

The duo reached the state park around 8 a.m., and by 9 a.m., they were holding "The Lucky Diamond," according to a statement from the Crater of Diamonds State Park. Frederick said he picked up the pearly white stone after spotting light reflecting off the ground only three feet from where he was standing.

Lauren said they were cautious not to get too excited until they figured out if the uncut diamond was the real deal.

"When we first found the diamond we kept looking up pictures on the Internet to make sure it was real and kept guessing what the weight would be," Lauren said in a statement. After finding the "Lucky Diamond," the pair walked around the park for another seven hours looking for another diamond, Lauren said.

According to the park, larger diamonds are sometimes found on the surface after rain washes the dirt away and exposes the heavier stones.

"Dan Frederick has proven, once again, that it is possible to find large, beautiful diamonds while surface searching," Betty Coors said in a statement.

The pair plans to keep the diamond.

ALSO BY PAUL SHERBURNE

The Lost Grotto
One Tree at a Time
The Box Boys
Lady Elba
Ebeemee Folk

About the Author

Growing up in the post-depression years of WWII, Paul Rogers Sherburne was the middle child in a family of three boys. His mother gave piano and violin lessons at home, and his father was a funeral director in a small family-owned business. He grew up in a small town (entire high school population just over 100) and spent much of his childhood in the forest engaged in exploration and games of fantasy. Favorite activities included spending summers at his grandparent's camp on a remote pond or being a guest at his great aunt's farm in the country. Most of his writing can be traced to these experiences.

Following graduation from high school and military service as an electronics technician in the US Navy (post-Korea and pre-Vietnam) he earned the first of three college degrees (mathematics, psychology and management), culminating in a doctorate from Michigan State University in 1968. A series of positions in university administration was followed by a twenty-year career as a small business owner and retail store planning consultant. Paul retired to Florida in the late 1990s to share time with his two brothers (snowbirds) and his parents. He played a lot of golf.

After a period of ten years and with the passing of his parents, he converted lifestyles to become a full-time RV'er. Now, in furtherance of the goal of periodically visiting his two daughters and grandchildren in Connecticut and Washington states while experiencing more of the country's scenery and people in between, he augmented his travel fund by returning to work full time. For five years he served in the Defense Department while working for the US Marine Corps in eastern North Carolina, and more recently the VA at the South Florida National Cemetery in Lake Worth. He is now retired and soon plans to get on with the traveling.

www.ingramcontent.com/pod-product-compliance
Lightning Source LLC
Chambersburg PA
CBHW051953220626
47052CB00004B/929